"It's about time you bull's-eye."

Porter picked up two sets of darts.

"I've never played darts before," Wendy said.

"Really? Could've fooled me." Porter's chuckle drifted into Wendy's ear as he stood behind her to correct her position. His arm snaked around her waist.

"What are you doing?" she whispered, when his breath feathered across the back of her neck.

"Showing you how to throw." He pulled her arm back and then thrust it forward. She released the dart and it sailed across the room, hitting the wall next to the board.

"You're not a very good teacher."

"Sorry, I'm better at other things."

She gazed up at Porter and the heat in his eyes burned her face and stole her breath.

Right now, she didn't care about her job or the investigation. All she wanted was to feel Porter's mouth on hers. She leaned forward.

"It's late. We'd better go." Porter stepped back suddenly and Wendy lost her balance. He steadied her, then escorted her to the door.

Wendy was too shocked to stop him.

Dear Reader,

A Cowboy of Her Own is the final book in The Cash Brothers series and it seems like just yesterday oldest brother Johnny Cash was roping in his sister's best friend. And now it's time for Porter Wagoner Cash to fall in love. Porter is the youngest of the Cash brothers and has taken his sweet time growing up.

But once he meets Wendy Chin, he's determined to prove he's no longer the live-for-today, worry-about-tomorrow-later guy that everyone believes he is. He'll have to do more than prove he has his act together to win over Wendy's parents, who want their daughter to marry a man of their choosing. Porter is determined to show Mr. and Mrs. Chin that his love for their daughter is strong enough to overcome cultural barriers and stand the test of time.

If you missed reading any of the previous Cash Brothers books—*The Cowboy Next Door* (July 2013), *Twins Under the Christmas Tree* (October 2013), *Her Secret Cowboy* (February 2014), *The Cowboy's Destiny* (May 2014) or *True Blue Cowboy* (August 2014)—you'll find links to order them at www.marinthomas.com as well as a list of all my Harlequin American Romance novels and my social media hangouts.

Happy Ever After...The Cowboy Way,

Marin

A COWBOY
OF HER OWN

MARIN THOMAS

Recycling programs
for this product may
not exist in your area.

ISBN-13: 978-0-373-75550-9

A Cowboy of Her Own

Copyright © 2015 by Brenda Smith-Beagley

This edition published by arrangement with Harlequin Books S.A.

For questions and comments about the quality of this book,
please contact us at CustomerService@Harlequin.com.

® and TM are trademarks of Harlequin Enterprises Limited or its
corporate affiliates. Trademarks indicated with ® are registered in the
United States Patent and Trademark Office, the Canadian Intellectual
Property Office and in other countries.

Printed in U.S.A.

Marin Thomas grew up in the Midwest, then attended college at the U of A in Tucson, Arizona, where she earned a BA in Radio-TV and played basketball for the Lady Wildcats. Following graduation she married her college sweetheart in the historical Little Chapel of the West in Las Vegas, Nevada. Recent empty nesters Marin and her husband now live in Texas, where cattle is king, cowboys are plentiful and pickups rule the road.

Books by Marin Thomas

HARLEQUIN AMERICAN ROMANCE

The Cash Brothers

The Cowboy Next Door
Twins Under the Christmas Tree
Her Secret Cowboy
The Cowboy's Destiny
True Blue Cowboy

Rodeo Rebels

Rodeo Daddy
The Bull Rider's Secret
A Rodeo Man's Promise
Arizona Cowboy
A Cowboy's Duty
No Ordinary Cowboy

Visit the Author Profile page at Harlequin.com for more titles

To Denise Hall...my Ohio-rockin', country-western-music-lovin' cowgirl posse leader! Your hard work, creativity and endless energy helped to make The Cash Brothers a bestselling series. Thank you for your friendship and for supporting my books. You keep me sane in this crazy business!

Chapter One

"Hey, Porter!"

Porter Wagoner Cash glanced up at the stands from the cowboy ready area at the Yuma Rodeo Fairgrounds and spotted the buckle bunnies waving signs with his name on them. He grinned at the familiar faces—girls he'd dated and flirted with. Sauntering closer to their section, he removed his hat. "Hello, ladies." The women giggled and preened for him. He wasn't the best-looking Cash brother—Conway held that honor—but his live-for-the-moment-worry-about-tomorrow-later motto attracted his share of beauties.

"You gonna win today, Porter?" A blonde with a smokin' hot body winked at him.

"Darlin', I'll do my best for you." He blew a kiss at the group, then winced when a sharp pain shot through his right shoulder. The old injury had flared up two weeks ago after he'd entered a bull-riding competition on a buddy's dare. At almost twenty-eight he was growing too old to play with bulls, but he'd rather ride the circuit on the weekends than sit by his lonesome in the bunkhouse at the family pecan farm.

"You comin' to the Horseshoe later?" a redhead named Michelle asked. Porter liked all women but he had a thing for redheads. His brother Buck had married one, and Destiny was a woman to be reckoned with.

"I'll be at the bar," Porter said. The Horseshoe was one of his regular hangouts. His brother Mack and his band, Cowboy Rebels, used to play there every other Saturday night. But now that Mack and his wife, Beth, had adopted a teenage boy and a preteen girl, his brother was too busy being a father to perform in bars.

"Will you save a dance for me?"

"Me, too."

"Me three."

"I'll dance with all of you." He loved country music, and there was nothing sweeter than holding a pretty girl close and shuffling her across a dance floor.

"Hey, Cash, you here alone?"

Porter glanced behind him. All-around cowboy C. J. Rodriguez—the Cash brothers' nemesis—walked in his direction.

"I'm the only Cash competing today."

"I guess your brothers are too busy being *daddies* to play with the big boys."

Porter stood a good three inches taller than the infamous bull rider. If his shoulder didn't ache so much, he'd wipe the smug smirk off the man's face. Who was he kidding? Out of all his siblings, Porter was the make-love-not-war brother. He used his mouth, not his fists, to settle disputes. "What's the matter, Rodriguez? Are you worried you won't find a woman to marry who'll put up with all your crap?"

"I'm never getting hitched." Rodriguez nodded to the cowboys standing a few yards away. "You still mourning your old flame?"

Porter couldn't stop himself from staring. Veronica

Patriot stood in the middle of the pack, her body plastered against a wet-behind-the-ears bronc buster.

Porter's eldest brother, Johnny, had warned him to steer clear of Veronica, but she'd reeled Porter in with her pretty blue eyes and sexy curves. For the first time in his life, he'd fallen hard for the woman. She'd done and said all the right things to make him believe she was just as in love with him, but it had been an act. She'd used him to make an old boyfriend jealous and when she'd succeeded, she'd left Porter in the dust. The only satisfaction he'd gotten from the whole experience was learning a few months later that the old boyfriend had kicked Veronica to the curb not long after they'd reunited.

"'Eat, Drink and Be Merry'…cowboy."

Rodriguez thought he was a real cutup, quoting Porter Wagoner song titles. Thanks to Porter's mother, who'd named her sons after country-and-western legends, he and his siblings had been teased all their lives. It didn't bother Porter too much anymore—except when jerks like Rodriguez ran off at the mouth. He fisted his hands to keep from grasping the man's Kevlar vest and shaking him.

"Hey, Cash!" Maxwell Black walked up to Porter. "A group of us are off-roading next weekend near Somerton. You wanna join us?"

Porter had gone through school with Max, and they'd stirred up their share of trouble in their teens. "I can't. I'm a working man now."

His friends gaped at him. "You got a real job?" Max asked.

"Yep." Porter had landed a position as a roughstock driver two months ago and had already made several runs.

Max shook his hand. "Congratulations, man. Where are you working?"

"I'm hauling bulls for Del Mar Rodeo Productions."

"Buddy Davidson is a big-time stock contractor," Max said. "How'd you land that gig?"

"Ran into Hank Martin at the Horseshoe Saloon back in February. He works for Davidson and he said Del Mar was hiring drivers to cover their spring and summer rodeo schedule."

Porter hadn't believed he had a chance in hell of getting the job, because the only thing he'd ever hauled had been lumber, but he'd left the bar that night and filled out one of the company's online applications.

A week later he was called in for an interview and given the job on the spot. Hank had spent a few minutes reciting the rules and showing Porter the paperwork for transporting livestock over state lines. The rest of his questions had been about Porter's family, particularly his mother, who'd been dead for more than a decade. It wasn't until the end of the interview that Hank had mentioned he'd known Porter's mother, Aimee, and had been sorry to hear she'd passed away.

It had been years since he'd held down a forty-hour-a-week job that wasn't seasonal work. Del Mar Rodeo was Porter's chance to prove to his siblings that he'd left his freewheeling days behind him and was committed to one day owning a ranch of his own.

I'll believe it when I see it. Johnny's voice echoed in Porter's head. How often had Johnny said, "C'mon, Porter, grow up. Life isn't always about having fun."

"We'll catch you later," Max said.

"Sounds good." Porter hefted his gear bag over his shoulder and made a beeline for the bronc-bustin' chutes. With his bum arm, he couldn't wrestle on his shirt, let alone a steer, so he'd entered the bareback competition, hoping he had a shot of making the top five.

"Ladies and gents, turn your attention to chute number three. Porter Cash is about to do battle with Starry Night." The fans stomped their boots on the bleachers, and Porter's buckle-bunny fan club flashed their posters with his name on them.

"Starry Night, you ready for a little fun?" Porter pulled on his riding glove then adjusted his spurs.

"You're the only cowboy I know who talks to a bronc like a pet dog."

"Speaking of mutts…don't you have anything better to do, Rodriguez, than follow me around like a lost puppy?" Porter zipped his Kevlar vest.

"And miss watching a Cash fall flat on his face?" The cowboy shook his head. "I don't think so."

"Tell me something," Porter said. "Are you just pissed that Shannon Douglas was a better bull rider than you or that she married Johnny?"

Rodriguez raised his hands in the air. "I'd rather go ten rounds with a nasty bull than take on Shannon."

"That's what I thought." Porter climbed the rails and settled a leg over the bronc. Starry Night decided he didn't like the extra weight on his back and reared. Porter dove for the rails and waited for the horse to settle down. He hoped he hadn't made a mistake in competing today. He didn't need a broken arm or leg before hitting the road Monday morning with a trailer full of bulls.

"Folks, this bronc doesn't think too highly of Porter Cash." The announcer's chuckle filled the stands.

The crowd quieted, their gazes riveted to Porter and the cantankerous gelding. When Starry Night stood still, Porter gave it another try and eased onto the horse's back. When he was certain the animal wouldn't object again, he wrapped the rope around his hand and secured his grip.

"Looks like our rider might be having second thoughts." The announcer startled Porter out of his reverie and he sucked in a deep breath, then nodded to the gateman.

The chute opened, and Starry Night catapulted into the arena, his back legs kicking out before his body cleared the gate. Porter held his seat and spurred, ignoring the ache in his shoulder when he raised his right arm high above his head. Starry Night's hooves hit the dirt hard, then the horse spun right, the move meant to unseat his rider. Not a chance. Porter wasn't going down that easy. He clenched his thighs against the bronc's girth and ignored the fire licking his strained muscles. Sweat stung his eyes, and his fingers grew numb from the stranglehold he had on the rope.

Porter braced himself for another spin and was caught off guard when the bronc reared. Only a superhero could have maintained his balance. His backside slid toward the horse's rump, and he clung to the rope like a man dangling off a cliff. But he was no match for Starry Night's power and he quit spurring. The bodies in the stands became a blur of color and the roar of the crowd faded to a muted drone. He'd lost this skirmish with the bronc, but the battle wasn't over until the dismount. He spotted an opening, but before he was able to release the rope the horse planted his front hooves in the dirt and sent Porter sailing into the air.

His injured shoulder hit the ground first, taking the brunt of his weight. For a split second his vision dimmed, then a bright light flashed inside his head, blinding him. He crawled to his hands and knees, the right side of his body numb, which messed up his balance. Halfway to his feet he pitched forward and did a face-plant in the dirt.

The ground reverberated beneath him as Starry Night continued to buck. When the pickup men released the flank strap, the bronc trotted out of the arena as if he was taking an afternoon stroll. Porter got to his feet and stumbled to the rails, where a helping hand yanked him to safety. He bent at the waist and gasped for air, willing the throb in his shoulder to subside.

"What did you do to tick that bronc off?"

Breathing hard enough to generate electricity, Porter wasn't sure if he imagined the feminine voice next to his ear or not. Dizzy with pain, he glanced to his right and discovered a pair of neatly pressed suit pants hugging slim hips that gave way to slender thighs and black high-heeled pumps. What woman in her right mind dressed in business attire to attend a rodeo?

He straightened, his six feet towering over her. He studied her teal silk blouse, slender, pale neck and smoky almond-shaped eyes. Other than the black eyeliner and pink lip gloss, she wore no makeup on her flawless skin.

She crossed her arms over her chest and arched a perfectly shaped eyebrow at him. "You don't remember me, do you?"

"You kind of look familiar." He racked his brain for a name. She wasn't a buckle bunny who traveled the circuit, but he couldn't remember where he'd run into her before.

"Wendy Chin."

He snapped his fingers. *Dixie's friend.* "You rode bulls with my sister a few summers ago."

"Rode *a* bull." She held up one finger—the oval-shaped nail as petite and delicate as her body.

"I remember you now. Your parents own the Yuma flower shop on Main Street."

"You're a hard man to track down," she said. "Do you have a minute to talk?"

"Sure." He had no idea what Wendy Chin wanted from him, but he wasn't about to turn down an invitation to chat with a pretty woman. Dixie insisted that her girlfriends were off-limits—not that Johnny had paid any attention to the warning. He'd married Shannon, but Porter and the rest of his brothers had heeded their sister's demand.

"Be right back." Porter walked over to the empty chute where he'd left his gear bag and removed his vest, spurs and riding glove, then slipped the duffel over his good shoulder and returned to Wendy's side. When the announcer's voice blasted through the sound system, introducing the next cowboy, he motioned for her to follow him to the livestock pens, where it would be easier to hear over bawling cows than loud music.

When they stepped outside, she said, "Let's get out of the sun." They crossed the gravel lot to a storage unit with an overhang wide enough for the two of them to fit under. For a woman who'd been born and raised in Arizona, her skin looked like fine porcelain instead of thick leather.

"Why have you been searching for me?" he asked.

"You work for Del Mar Rodeo."

"I knew my family was excited that I'd finally landed

a permanent job, but I didn't expect Dixie to broadcast the news to her friends."

"Dixie didn't tell me."

Wendy's sober eyes told him that their chat had a purpose and it wasn't to catch up on old times. "Why does it matter to you that I work for Del Mar?"

A tinge of pink swept across her cheeks. "I'm your copilot to Grand Junction, Colorado."

He banged his palm against the side of his head, thinking dust must have clogged his ears. "Copilot?"

"I work for American Livestock Insurance, and Del Mar Rodeo is our biggest client. We do a ride-along once a year with one of the stock haulers."

"Neither Buddy nor Hank mentioned that I'd have a passenger on this trip."

"It's not a big deal. I just need to document the number of hours you drive each day, how many breaks you take and how you care for the animals."

If it wasn't a big deal, why hadn't he been told she'd be going on the trip with him?

Look on the bright side.

There was a bright side?

It'll be fun to have a companion on the trip. "I'm picking up the trailer at seven Monday morning."

"I'll meet you at the pecan farm." She frowned. "Is it okay to leave my car there until we return?"

"Sure."

"I'll see you then."

Wendy wove through the parked cars and hopped in one of those gas-efficient vehicles that looked as though it belonged in a Matchbox car collection. Not until she drove off did his arm begin to throb again. Unless he wanted Wendy to put in her report that his bum shoulder interfered with his ability to drive the rig, he'd better hightail it home and ice the injury.

No way was he losing his job over something a nosy claims adjuster—a pretty one at that—put in her report.

WENDY WAS STILL blushing after her talk with Porter at the rodeo. Why her friend's brother made her nervous was anybody's guess. Sure, he was good-looking—all the Cash brothers were handsome—but Porter wasn't her type. According to Dixie, he didn't want to grow up. He was more interested in partying and working only when he needed money to fill the gas tank or treat a buckle bunny to a night on the town. Wendy was Porter's polar opposite. She was a go-getter and a stay-later at the job.

Even though they were different, Wendy had felt a tingle in her stomach when Porter's gaze roamed over her body. She preferred serious, career-minded men, but there was something appealing about Porter's laid-back attitude—not that she would ever do anything unprofessional with him.

As if you'd ever get the chance.

A girl could indulge in a fantasy or two, couldn't she? Porter gravitated toward the well-endowed buckle bunny cheerleaders who screamed his name at rodeos. *Voluptuous* was not an adjective anyone would use to describe Wendy. Thanks to her Asian genes, her petite body lacked pronounced curves.

She pulled into the parking lot behind her parents' flower shop and entered through the back door. "Hi, Mom." Her mother was hard at work. "Are these the centerpieces for the ladies' auxiliary banquet?"

"Where have you been? I thought you were helping me today."

"I had to take care of a few things at the office." Wendy hadn't told her parents she'd be riding along with one of Buddy Davidson's drivers because they'd worry. They agonized over everything—her safety, her diet, her job and her single status. Lately she'd begun wishing she didn't live next to them. They shared a duplex that her parents had purchased in the '80s. Although the low rent allowed her to put a substantial amount of money into savings each month, Wendy yearned for her privacy. Whenever she suggested she look for a new apartment, her parents became upset and changed the subject.

Wendy threw on an apron. "How many arrangements do you need to make?"

"Twenty-five." Her mother pointed to the table against the wall. "I've finished ten."

Wendy selected several sprigs of greenery and copied her mother's design. When she finished, she held up the vase. "Good enough?"

"Perfect."

They worked in comfortable silence for a half hour before Wendy spoke. "I'm traveling on business next week."

"Where to?"

"Colorado. I'm documenting livestock drivers for our annual report." No need to explain that she'd be monitoring just one driver. Her parents were old-fashioned and wouldn't approve of her being alone with a man, even if that man was her friend's brother.

"You've never done that before."

"My boss believes it's important that I have a good

understanding of the transport process when I'm working claims for missing or injured livestock." The less her mother knew the better. Wendy didn't want word getting out that American Livestock Insurance was doing their own investigation into Del Mar's missing bulls after the sheriff's search had stalled out.

Buddy Davidson had been with American Livestock for fifteen years and had never had a bull go missing until a few months ago, when he'd filed claims for three. If that wasn't suspicious enough, Wendy had interviewed Glen Fenderblast, Buddy's ranching neighbor, and he'd said that Buddy had his eye on buying a bull named Happy Hour worth $1.2 million. The payout on Buddy's missing roughstock would cover half the cost of the new bull. Before Carl Evans, Wendy's boss, cut Buddy a check, he wanted to make certain that Del Mar Rodeo wasn't trying to swindle its insurance company. The ride-along was their last chance to uncover any information that might be useful to the sheriff's case.

Wendy had her doubts that Porter was involved in any illegal activity since he'd been hired right after Buddy had reported the lost bulls, but she had to be objective and look closely at everyone who worked for Del Mar Rodeo.

"Is there a promotion in this for you?" her mother asked.

Wendy had been promoted a little over a year ago, a fact that her parents frequently forgot. "I doubt Carl is ready for me to take over his job."

As an only child and a daughter, she felt the weight of her parents' high expectations of her. The constant pressure to climb the proverbial career ladder was overwhelming. She wanted more out of life than working twelve-hour days.

"Is the company paying for your motel room?"

"Yes." Wendy finished a second arrangement and placed the vase on the table.

"When are you leaving?"

"Monday morning. I won't return until the following Sunday."

"You'll check in with us." It wasn't a request or suggestion—it was an order.

"I'm twenty-six years old. I shouldn't have to report my daily whereabouts and activities to my parents."

"Then find a husband and get married so he can worry about you."

Grrr...

"By the way, your father's taking one of his suppliers to dinner tonight and he'd like you to join them."

Not again. Wendy wished her dad would stop playing matchmaker. Even though her parents had been born in the United States, they clung to their traditional beliefs and wanted their only child to marry a hardworking, dedicated Chinese man so there would be no cultural clashes in the family. Wendy walked a fine line between two worlds, struggling to balance embracing the American way of life while still respecting her Chinese ancestry.

Unbeknownst to her parents, she had lost her heart in college to a classmate at Arizona State University. Tyler had been spontaneous, adventurous and exciting. They'd dated almost a year when Wendy found out by accident that he was engaged to a girl in his hometown of Tucson. The two-timing jerk had broken her heart and left her gun-shy when it came to serious relationships.

After graduating from college, she'd returned to Yuma and dated Asian men her father had selected for her. Polite, educated and dedicated to their careers, the men were everything her parents believed important. But none of them had made her heart stumble or her pulse quicken. Wendy wanted to marry a man she fell in love with, not a man her parents believed she'd be compatible with.

Wendy had grown up watching her parents toil in the flower shop seven days a week, year after year, and that wasn't the life she dreamed of. She deserved more from a marriage than a working partnership. And she yearned for a man she could have fun with. The men she'd dated would never put their children or wives ahead of their careers. Wendy didn't want to be number two in her husband's heart. She wanted to be his top priority.

Porter's image flashed before her eyes. He knew how to have fun. She'd be lying if she didn't admit she was looking forward to traveling with him. But she wasn't so naive as to believe anything could come of a week on the road with the cowboy.

"Make your father happy," her mother said. "Go to dinner with him."

Fine. "When do I need to be ready?"

"Seven-thirty. And wear that aqua dress you bought last spring. That looks nice on you."

"Can you handle the rest of the arrangements if I grab a quick shower?"

"Go ahead. I've already done half of them myself."

Feeling a tad guilty for leaving her mom with a table full of empty vases—but not too guilty since she'd been coerced into accepting a blind date—Wendy kissed her mother's cheek and left the shop. As she drove across town, she lectured herself. As much as she anticipated the upcoming trip with Porter, she needed to keep her priorities straight and focus on finding information that would help locate Buddy's missing bulls.

Time would tell if she uncovered any evidence that pointed to Porter. For Dixie's sake—and maybe a little bit for her sake, too—she hoped her friend's brother was on the up and up.

Chapter Two

"Porter!"

"In here!" Porter stuffed the last pair of briefs into the duffel bag resting on the bed in the bunkhouse. The door opened and in walked Johnny. "It's Sunday night. Why aren't you home watching TV with Shannon and Addy?"

"Mack said you were heading out on a weeklong run tomorrow, and we haven't had a chance to talk in a while."

"Checking up on me?" Because of their age difference, the eldest Cash sibling was more of a father than a brother to Porter.

Johnny tossed his cowboy hat on the table and gestured to the rodeo posters on the wall. "We had some good parties in here, didn't we?"

"Yeah, we did. Then you and everyone else got hitched and left me all by my lonesome."

"I doubt you feel lonely when you don't have to wait in line for a shower and you can watch whatever television program you want." Johnny picked up the remote and pointed it at the flat screen. The Nickelodeon channel came on. "You're hanging out with the twins too much."

"Mig and Javi are the only ones who visit me." Conway and Isi were busy taking care of their new twin daughters and the boys had turned to Porter for attention.

Johnny ran his hand over the back of the sofa, and dog hair stuck to his fingers. "I guess Bandit's been a regular visitor in here."

"He only comes inside when it storms."

"It hasn't rained in over thirty days," Johnny said.

"What do you care if I let the dog sleep in here? It's not like you have to clean the place anymore."

"You're right. Better the dog in the bunkhouse than a bunch of buckle bunnies."

"Hey, no matter what Conway says, I haven't let a girl stay overnight in the bunkhouse since Isi and the twins moved to the farm. I know better."

"We shouldn't have let our Wednesday night poker game fall by the wayside."

Porter emptied his sock drawer into the duffel. "If you guys would stop procreating, you might have a free day to play cards."

"The love bug will bite you one of these days," Johnny said. "You wait and see."

"I've got more important things to do than worry about finding the right woman to settle down with." Besides, how was he supposed to meet the perfect lady when he drove a stock trailer all day?

Johnny stared him square in the eye. "You think you'll keep this job long-term?" He was really asking if Porter would grow bored of transporting bulls and quit as he'd done with previous jobs.

"You want an honest answer or you want me to make something up?"

"Honest."

Porter sat on the bed and expelled a heavy breath. "I think so."

"You *think* so?"

"Sometimes I wish I'd given college a try." He'd never talked to his brothers about the restless feeling he'd battled daily since graduating from high school.

"Why didn't you?" Johnny asked. "You made decent grades and with our family's situation you'd have qualified for financial aid to help pay the tuition."

"I didn't know what I wanted to study. But I've been thinking—"

"That's dangerous."

"Ha-ha. Buck's dream of owning a car-repair business came true, so why can't I make my dream come true?"

"What's your dream?"

"I've always wanted a piece of land to call my own."

"You mean like a ranch?"

Porter nodded. "We grew up on the pecan farm, but it's really Conway's now. One day you and Shannon are going to run the Triple D. And I bet it's not long before Mack buys in to a partnership at the Black Jack Mountain Dude Ranch."

"If you had your own ranch, what would you raise?"

"Bucking stock." Porter recalled the strength and talent of Starry Night at yesterday's rodeo. "Broncs."

"You have a lot of competition in the area," Johnny said.

"The rodeo circuit keeps expanding. There's room for more good horses."

"Have you thought about where you'd buy this ranch?"

"There's a property for sale in the Fortuna Foothills." The land was east of Yuma but still considered part of the metropolitan area. He wouldn't be far from his siblings if he moved out there.

"How many acres?"

"Twenty-five. Enough for a handful of horses."

"If you want it bad, let's find a way to make it happen."

It was just like Johnny to step in and take charge. Porter appreciated the support, but he intended to figure out the future on his own. He knew for sure that he didn't want to haul rodeo bulls the rest of his life, but he needed to prove to himself that he could stick with the job or investing in a business would be a waste of his money and effort.

"Thanks for the offer, but my first priority is to do my job well and not give Buddy Davidson a reason to fire me."

"Are you nervous about this trip?" Johnny always sensed when one of his brothers was uneasy.

"A little. It's twelve hours from here to Grand Junction, Colorado, where I pick up the bulls." His previous runs had been across southern Arizona—no more than five hours each way. This trip would last an entire week.

"What has you worried?" Johnny asked. "The roughstock growing restless or you?"

"It won't be me." Porter grinned. "I've got company on this trip."

"Who?"

"Remember Dixie's friend Wendy Chin?"

"Sure. She was part of that crazy group of girls who helped Shannon promote her bull-riding tour a few summers ago."

"Wendy works for American Livestock Insurance and she's coming along for the ride."

"Never heard of an insurance rep doing that before."

Neither had Porter, but there wasn't much he could do about the situation. "She's monitoring my driving habits and how I handle the bulls."

"I guess it doesn't matter why she's going on the trip as long as you remember she's Dixie and Shannon's friend. Keep—"

"My hands to myself. I know." Johnny acted as if Porter planned to jump Wendy's bones as soon as she climbed into the truck cab. "Wendy isn't my type."

"Good. Keep it that way."

The last thing Porter wanted was to become tangled up with Wendy Chin—an educated career woman with a mind of her own. Her diminutiveness might bring out a man's protective instincts, but he suspected Wendy could handle almost anything and anyone she crossed paths with.

"When are you leaving in the morning?" Johnny asked.

"As soon as Wendy gets here. I told her she could leave her car at the farm."

"Have her park it behind the barn so the twins don't mess with it."

"Good thinking." He waited for Johnny to grab his hat and mosey along, but his brother didn't budge. "Something else on your mind?"

"Not really."

Porter laughed. "Spit it out."

"I guess it's more difficult than I expected."

"What's that?"

"Accepting that all my brothers have grown up and they don't need me anymore."

Porter smothered a smile behind his hand. The strongest brother, the one who'd defended his siblings against playground bullies and as a result had made multiple trips to the principal's office, looked like a lost kid. "It doesn't matter how old we become," Porter said. "You'll always be our big brother and the go-to guy for advice."

Johnny released a loud breath. "I'm glad, because all I've ever wanted is for my siblings to be happy."

"It was tough when Grandma and Grandpa died, but I wasn't scared, because I knew you'd be there for me." Porter studied his boots before looking Johnny in the eye. "Remember when Mom died? You were worried about me because I didn't want to talk about it."

"I remember."

"The reason I didn't say much is because I didn't feel sad and I thought I was supposed to. Then I found you crying down by the pond and I felt guilty that I couldn't even shed a tear for my own mother."

Porter had never told a soul about his eldest brother's crying jag because he'd been so shaken at the sight. That night he'd realized that Johnny wasn't a superhero but a human being. "You were the family rock, Johnny. Even before Mom passed on, we turned to you when we needed help." Porter shoved a hand through his hair and paced in front of the TV. "I pretended Mom's passing didn't affect me because I didn't want you to worry about me."

"Mom's death did bother you."

"Not for the reasons you think." Porter shrugged. "I never got to ask about my father. I know the rest of you had had conversations with her about your fathers, but she and I never had that talk."

"Did you find out his name?" Johnny asked.

"Nope." Porter laughed the sound bitter. "And I actually wanted to know who he was."

"I'm sorry. But maybe it was for the best."

"Maybe." When his brothers had reached out to their biological fathers, they'd been rejected. "I'm slowly coming to grips with the possibility that I'll never know who my dad is."

"What about the stuff Grandma left in the attic?"

"I went through the boxes a couple of years ago. There's no information about any of our fathers."

"If you decide to search for him, I'll help in any way I can."

"Thanks." Porter figured his brother would remain in the bunkhouse forever if he didn't nudge him toward the door. "I need to finish packing."

Johnny put on his hat. "Don't forget to text Dixie when you arrive in Grand Junction. She'll send out a search party if you don't."

He wouldn't forget, because he didn't want to be embarrassed in front of Wendy if his brothers showed up out of the blue to check on him.

Why do you care what Wendy thinks?

He didn't care. "I'll keep Dixie informed of my whereabouts."

Johnny opened the bunkhouse door. "Does Dixie know Wendy's going with you?"

"Not unless Wendy told her." If the two had talked, Porter was sure his sister would have warned him to mind his manners with her friend. "Say hi to Shannon and give Addy a hug from Uncle Porter."

"Will do. Drive safe."

Once the door shut behind Johnny, Porter sprawled across the couch. He hated that one of his sister's girlfriends would be monitoring his every move and groaned when he thought of spending a week with the no-nonsense woman. He closed his eyes and conjured up an image of Wendy in her suit pants and silk blouse.

This was going to be the longest road trip of his life.

"YOUR TRUCK SMELLS brand-new," Wendy said after she climbed into Porter's Dodge Ram.

"I bought it three months ago. It's my new babe magnet," he joked.

Babe magnet aside, Wendy marveled at how a rodeo bum/livestock hauler could afford a new pickup. Maybe he'd saved for years to cover the down payment. Or maybe Buddy Davidson had paid Porter a bonus when he'd signed on to work at Del Mar Rodeo. Or…maybe Porter had been told if he asked no questions and did his job well he'd receive a kickback after Buddy collected the insurance money from the missing bulls. Wendy had a tough time believing her friend's brother was a criminal.

"Wave goodbye to the twins." Porter nodded to Conway's sons, standing on the porch in their pajamas.

She waggled her fingers out the window. "What are they doing up at five-thirty in the morning on a school day?"

"Their twin sisters' crying probably woke them. The walls in the farmhouse are pretty thin."

Dixie had posted a cute picture of the girls to her Facebook page the day Isi gave birth to them.

Porter started the truck, shifted gear, then honked as he drove out of the yard.

"I bet Isi doesn't get much sleep with infant twins and two rambunctious six-year-olds to take care of."

"The boys being in school full-time helps. During the day Conway focuses on the farm, then when Mig and Javi get off the bus, he keeps them out of Isi's hair."

"I doubt Conway and Isi have much time to themselves."

"Every couple of weeks I have a sleepover in the bunkhouse with the boys so their parents can have a date night."

The scent of Porter's cologne filled the cab and the earthy smell distracted Wendy. She should be asking questions about his job, not his family. "Sounds as if you like being an uncle."

He chuckled, the gravelly noise rolling over her skin and making her shiver. "Are you cold?" He switched off the air conditioner. The fact that he noticed made it even more difficult to focus on her job.

"How long have you been working for an insurance company?" He turned onto the highway.

"Four years. I hired on with American Livestock after college."

"I'm sure Dixie mentioned it, but where did you go to school?"

"Arizona State University. I graduated from the W. P. Carey School of Business." Was it her imagination or were Porter's knuckles turning white against the steering wheel? "Did you go to college?"

"I couldn't decide what I wanted to study. Then I got caught up in rodeoing with my brothers—" he shrugged

"—and never ended up registering for any classes at the junior college."

"I was surprised when I saw your name on Buddy's roster of drivers. Last I'd heard you were working with Mack at the Black Jack Mountain Dude Ranch."

"About twenty hours a week," he said. "I filled in when they needed an extra hand."

"Do you like cowboying?"

"I do. And I liked socializing with the ranch guests."

That didn't shock her. Of all the Cash brothers, Porter was the friendliest—former Mr. Popular in high school. She'd rarely seen him walk the halls alone and students had always gathered at his locker between classes. And he never sat by himself in the cafeteria, which made him taking a job that required driving long hours *alone* odd.

"If you enjoyed the dude ranch, how did you end up going to work for Del Mar?" she asked.

"I'd been on the lookout for a permanent job for a while."

"Was the position advertised in the newspaper? Online? Did you hear about it from a friend?"

Porter's eyebrows drew together. "Actually, it was the strangest thing. I ran into Hank Martin at a bar. He said Buddy was hiring drivers and suggested I apply."

Wendy knew that Hank Martin was Buddy's right-hand man and handled the rodeo scheduling.

Porter nodded to the iPad Wendy had opened on her lap. "Are you documenting my answers on that thing?"

"No."

"Do you ask all the drivers you ride with the same questions?"

Porter's inquisitiveness would only get her in trouble and she didn't want to lie any more than she had to, so she changed the subject. "How many hours of training did Del Mar provide you with?"

"None. Hank asked if I'd ever driven a rig before and I said no but that I'd hauled my share of horse trailers. That seemed to satisfy him."

Had Buddy known that Hank had sent Porter out with little to no training? Rodeo bulls were expensive, especially those with winning records. It didn't make sense for Hank to trust the bulls with an inexperienced driver.

"How many trips have you gone on?" she asked.

"Twelve. They were short runs. Didn't have any trouble."

When Porter reached the Yuma city limits, he turned onto the county road that would take them to Buddy's ranch. Fifteen miles later he parked the pickup next to the hay barn.

Hoping she wouldn't run into Buddy and have to make up a lie as to why she hadn't informed him that she was tagging along with Porter, she said, "I'll wait in the pickup while you get the keys to the stock trailer."

"The keys are in the trailer. Hank and Buddy left for Idaho yesterday. They're checking out a new bull at a ranch up there." Porter grabbed their overnight bags and stowed them in the cab of the trailer.

Wendy stood aside while Porter inspected the tires and made sure the latch on the trailer was secure. "Do you check in with Buddy each day when you're on the road?"

"No. If I report to anyone, it's Hank." He pulled out his phone.

"I'll need to know if Hank asks you to do anything unusual on this trip."

"What do you mean unusual?"

"Change your route. Make an extra stop somewhere."

"Hey." Porter held up his hands. "I don't want to get caught in the middle of anything between you and Hank or you and Buddy. I just want to do my job." After testing the latch a second time, he opened the passenger door for her. "There's no step up."

How was she supposed to get into the cab? Even if she took a running leap, she wouldn't be able to dive onto the floor.

"I'll give you a boost." Porter cupped his hands. "Put your foot in here and grab the handhold."

She stowed her iPad in her purse, then lifted her leg and set her boot in his hands. Before she'd prepared herself, he hoisted her into the air. She teetered off balance and made a valiant swipe at the handle inside the passenger door, but missed and pitched forward. She saw the top of the cab coming at her head and braced herself, but Porter's hands vanished from beneath her boot and she fell backward into his arms.

Oh, my.

Her breath caught and it wasn't because she'd slammed into Porter's chest and had the wind knocked out of her—it was because his grip had tightened on her fanny. Their faces were inches apart, and if she dipped her head a tiny bit...

He set her on the ground, then moved his hands from her bottom to her waist. "You okay?"

She could get used to the feel of Porter's hands on her body. She shook her head and the lusty thoughts scattered.

"You're not okay?" he asked. "Did you knock your head on the door?"

"No. I'm fine." She retreated a step.

If you don't get your act together you're going to blow this assignment.

Wendy believed her boss had put her in charge of this investigation because he trusted her and she didn't want to let him down.

"We have a long drive today," he said. "You ready to try and get into the cab again?"

"I'll do it on my own." She braced her foot against the front tire and pushed off—this time she snagged the handle and pulled herself into the cab.

Porter closed the door, then hopped in behind the wheel. When he backed away from the barn, he spoke. "Can I ask you a personal question?"

"Depends on the question."

"What's your waist size?"

Her mouth opened, then she snapped it closed.

"I'm guessing you don't get asked that very often."

"No, I don't." *Good Lord.* "Porter." She pulled in a steadying breath. "My waist size is none of your business." His grin exasperated her. "I realize we already know each other, but maybe I need to remind you that this isn't a joyride or a vacation for me."

His smile faded. "No, ma'am, you don't need to remind me at all." He stared out the windshield. "You can be sure I'll keep my hands to myself."

Great. She'd offended him. Now she'd be fortunate if he spoke two words to her the rest of the way to Colorado.

Chapter Three

What the heck was taking Wendy so long? Porter stared at the restroom door outside the mom-and-pop gas station on the outskirts of Flagstaff. They'd driven only five hours and had made three pit stops already. The first one to gas up before they left Yuma. The second to buy snacks in Phoenix, because he'd grown tired of listening to Wendy's stomach growl. And now a potty break. At the rate they were traveling, they wouldn't make Grand Junction until ten o'clock tonight.

He checked his cell phone for messages—none. Then he eyed the gas-station minimart, wondering how the building had remained standing when the outer walls sagged and the roof looked as if it might blow off with the next gust of wind. The owner could make more money than the property was worth if he sold the antique tin signs decorating the stucco facade. Drink Coca-Cola—Delicious And Refreshing hung next to the door, and below that was a Sinclair sign with the green dinosaur. On the opposite side of the door hung an old Mobilgas plaque with its winged horse. The faded black letters of Freedom Perfect Motor Oil Sold Here ran across the top of the building. Two red-white-and-blue Esso gas pumps—one regular and one diesel—lay on their sides in the dirt across the lot. A burn barrel served as a garbage can and sat between the newer gas pumps out front.

Tired of waiting in the hot sun, Porter pushed himself off the truck fender and went back into the snack shop.

The bell on the door announced his arrival and the clerk named Betty glanced up from the magazine in her hands. "You forget something?"

"I'm waiting for my copilot to finish in the rest-room." It didn't appear that Betty had budged from her stool behind the counter since he'd bought a lot-tery ticket from her twenty minutes ago. She shoved her hand inside a Cheetos bag and grabbed a cheese puff, then chomped on it like a hamster before turning the magazine page with an orange thumb and forefinger.

He wandered over to the newsstand and selected the local paper from three days ago to read the headlines: *When Push Cames to Shove, Elderly Man Lost Foot-ing. Grandmother Inspires Orphans to "Create" Fam-ily Trees. Big Burrito Man Abandons Truck, Dreams.*

The burrito man's story intrigued Porter, but before he had a chance to read the copy, a loud thump startled him. He glanced at Betty, but her head remained bur-ied in the gossip rag.

Thump. Thump. Thump.

The noise sounded as if it came from behind the wall next to Porter. "Did you hear that?"

Betty's hand froze inside the Cheetos bag. "Hear what?"

Thump. Thump.

"That sound." He pointed to the wall.

"The restroom is on the other side," Betty said.

Wendy.

"Key doesn't always work. Your friend might be stuck in there."

Unbelievable. "How long were you going to let her sit in there before you went to check on her?"

Betty stared as if he'd grown two heads.

"Never mind." Porter hurried outside and banged his fist on the bathroom door. "Wendy? You okay?"

"The key's stuck in the lock."

She didn't sound panicked, which surprised him. The women he'd known would have pitched a hissy fit by now if they'd gotten trapped inside a stinky gas-station latrine.

"Hang on!" He went into the store. "Do you have a screwdriver? Any kind of tool set?"

"What would I need with a screwdriver?" Betty asked.

"The restroom key is stuck in the lock, and I need to remove the door handle."

"You can't deface the property."

"This place is already defaced." He swallowed a curse word. By the time he and Wendy hit the road again another half hour would be wasted. "I'll reattach the door handle once I get her out."

Betty pried her backside off the stool and walked through the store. "There might be some tools on the endcap over here." She pointed an orange finger.

Sure enough. Porter opened the kit and removed the screwdriver. He took one step but stopped when Betty blocked his path. "You gotta pay for that."

He opened his mouth to argue with her, then decided not to waste his breath and handed her a five-dollar bill from his wallet. "Answer me one question," he said.

"Why does the restroom lock from the inside with a key?" That made no sense.

"Don't ask me. I just work here."

Porter went outside and rapped his knuckles on the door. "I'm going to remove the handle."

Wendy didn't say anything, and he became concerned that she'd passed out from the putrid fumes inside. He pressed the edge of the screwdriver into the latch at the base of the knob and jiggled it. The hardware was ancient and pulled right off. Next, he loosened the screws, then removed the mounting plate. "Hang on. I'm almost done." He poked his finger inside the hole, scraping his knuckle. Ignoring his bloody finger, he pushed the latch aside, then shoved the door open.

He wasn't sure what he expected to find inside the windowless graffiti-covered compartment with a chipped ceramic sink and condom wrappers littering the floor, but it sure wasn't Wendy perched on top of the toilet tank, texting away on her phone.

"Thanks for freeing me." She hopped off the toilet, inched past him and stepped outside, where she sucked in a breath of fresh air. "We should exchange phone numbers. If that happens again, I'll be able to text you." She marched to the truck, a strip of toilet paper stuck to the heel of her shoe fluttering in the air like a kite tail.

Her nonchalant attitude confounded Porter. Manipulating the jammed key was difficult when it was connected to a bike chain that had been padlocked to an old hubcap.

To hell with this. Cheetos Betty could figure it out. Porter replaced the outside knob then returned to the store. "I can't get the key out of the lock. You'll have to call a repairman."

Betty's head remained buried in the magazine, but she waved her orange fingers in the air, signaling that she'd heard him.

When Porter got into the truck cab, Wendy was working on her iPad. He glanced at the floor and noticed she'd removed the TP from her shoe. "I can't believe it."

She looked up from the screen. "Believe what?"

"You were just sitting there calm as can be, texting on your phone when I opened the restroom door."

"I was making good use of the time by checking work emails."

He stared, dumbfounded.

"I told you this isn't a vacation for me, Porter. I have accounts that I need to manage while we're traveling."

"You're a girl. You should have been distraught and panic-stricken." And she was supposed to jump into his arms and smother his face with kisses of gratitude once he'd freed her—that's how it played out in the movies.

"I'm not like most girls."

No kidding. He started the truck, then merged onto the highway. "We're not stopping again until we hit Durango or Silverton."

"That's fine." Wendy set aside her iPad and dug through the bag of snacks on the seat. She unwrapped a candy bar and said, "You're shaking your head again."

"I'll never understand women."

"At least you're smart enough to admit it. Most men assume women can't function without them. The truth is we can do everything they can and often better."

"I didn't see you free yourself from the bathroom."

"I would have figured a way out."

"Okay, smart lady. If I hadn't been there, how would you have gotten out of that jam?"

"I would have called nine-one-one."

Porter shut up and focused on his driving.

THE TRUCK HIT a bump, and Wendy's eyes popped open. "What happened?"

"Sorry. I didn't see the pothole in the pavement," Porter said.

She pressed the back of her hand against her mouth and yawned, waiting for her blurry eyes to focus. She wasn't used to wearing her contact lenses more than ten hours a day. As soon as she arrived home from work, she switched to her glasses. "It's late, isn't it?"

"Almost ten."

The cab was dark and she couldn't make out his features, but she heard the frustration in his voice. Their unexpected delay at the gas station earlier in the afternoon had put a kink in his driving schedule.

"You didn't actually plan on picking up the bulls tonight, did you?" The thought of the animals stuck inside a trailer until morning seemed cruel.

"No, but I wanted to have a little fun before I went to bed."

"Do you always hit up the bars and women when you're on the road?" She swallowed a groan. She was the same age as Porter, but she sounded like a crotchety old woman.

"As far as I know, when I'm off the clock it's not against company policy to have a beer or a dance with a pretty girl. Do you have a problem with that?"

"Forget I asked." Wendy wanted to get to the motel,

enjoy a soak in the tub and then drift off to sleep—after she checked her email.

"If I go out for a beer, will the information end up in your report?"

"What do mean?"

"Are you documenting my after-hours activities on this trip?"

"No." She tapped her fingernail against the armrest, willing the next ten miles to pass quickly.

"What do you do when you're off the clock?" he asked.

She laughed. "When is that?"

"You don't work 24/7…do you?"

"No, but there's always email and phone calls to catch up on."

"Surely your clients know you have a life outside of your job."

"Maybe, but livestock disasters strike whenever and wherever with no respect for the human workweek."

"There's no blizzard or dust storm affecting cows or horses tonight. What do you say we stretch our legs and let loose for a couple of hours before we check into a motel?"

A couple of hours—was he nuts? "If you drink and drive, I'll have to put it my report."

He flashed his pearly whites. "Then I'll be the designated driver."

"Get serious, Porter."

He frowned. "I am serious."

She opened her mouth to argue with him but changed her mind—until she caught him shaking his head. "What?" she asked.

"It's weird that you and my sister are friends."

"Why is it weird?"

"Dixie was rebellious but I doubt you ever went against your parents' wishes."

She didn't care for the critical tone in his voice, but bit her tongue. It would be cruel to argue that she respected her parents when Dixie and her brothers grew up without a mother and a father.

"Dixie gave my grandparents fits in junior high when she snuck off with Tanner Hamilton. They grounded her, but she kept leaving the house to be with him. My brothers and I followed her one night. Turns out she and Tanner had entered a dance competition and they were practicing in his family's garage."

Wendy knew that. "Glen Smith asked me to be his dance partner for the contest."

"You snuck out of your house, too?"

She hadn't dared disobey her parents. They would have been horrified if she'd met a boy late at night. She recalled sitting in the school cafeteria, listening to Dixie, Shannon and the other girls laugh and joke about the fun they'd had with the boys.

"I had to tell Glen I couldn't be his dance partner."

"Why not?"

She waved a hand in the air. "My parents wouldn't have approved."

"Did you have to follow a lot of rules growing up?" He chuckled. "Heck, after our grandparents went to bed at nine o'clock we'd sneak out and meet up with the Stockton brothers and party out in the desert."

"No parties for me," she said. Her parents hadn't needed to set boundaries with her. The dos and don'ts had been implied. Come to think of it, Wendy couldn't remember her father or mother ever raising their voices at her. Their preferred method of discipline had been giving her the *look*. The disappointment and censure in their eyes had affected her far more than if they'd grounded her.

"I think Grandma Ada and Grandpa Ely knew we ran wild after hours, but they were old and too tired to chase us down. And we never broke the law, except for the underage drinking."

"Dixie doesn't talk about your mother much."

"She wasn't around very often and when she was, she acted like one of us. I remember asking to borrow her car and she told me to check with my grandfather. It was as if she didn't consider us her kids."

"Dixie loved your grandmother."

"Yeah, it was tough on her when Grandma Ada died. The two used to spend hours in the barn making soaps from the family recipes."

Wendy wished she had a memory of doing something special with her mother—besides arranging flowers. But her mother and father were always busy in the shop. If Wendy had ever complained, her parents made her feel guilty, insisting they were toiling away for her future. It was difficult for her to be angry with them after they'd help pay for her college education.

"Who knows where I'd be now if I'd been raised by a mother and a father," Porter said.

If you'd been raised by my parents, you wouldn't have had nearly the fun you had on the farm. And I guarantee you wouldn't be driving a livestock truck.

Hoping to divert the conversation away from her childhood, she asked, "What are your hobbies?"

"Just rodeo. There's nothing like the rush of competing against a bull or bronc."

"Dixie said you and your brothers used to sneak onto your neighbor's property and ride his cows."

"Fred Pendleton and his wife, Millie, never had kids of their own and they ratted on me and my brothers every chance they got."

"What did your grandparents do?"

"Not much until Conway and Buck got caught letting Pendleton's prized heifer out of the pasture. The old man called social services and told them that our grandparents were too old to raise a bunch of hooligans and we should be taken away from them."

"That was mean."

"A lady from child welfare services stopped by the farm and threatened to put us all in different foster homes and it scared us kids bad enough that we quit playing pranks on the neighbors."

Wendy couldn't imagine the Cash siblings being split up. They were a tight-knit family who looked out for one another.

"What kind of trouble did you get into during your teens?" Porter asked.

Wendy was embarrassed to admit she'd been a Goody Two-shoes. "I broke curfew once." She'd been an hour late returning home from choir rehearsal. When she'd gone out to the school parking lot, she'd discovered a flat tire on her car. A teacher had offered to help, but she'd been determined to change the tire herself. The teacher had remained with her in the lot, cheering her on until she'd succeeded. And before he let her leave, he made her drive around until he was satisfied the tire wouldn't fall off.

"Did your parents ground you?"

"No." After she'd explained the emergency they'd

understood. But they'd still given her that *look* because she hadn't phoned them to say she'd be late.

"You felt guilty for weeks afterward."

She laughed. "Yes."

"I admit I was a goof-off in my younger years," he said. "But I've changed."

Wendy didn't comment.

"Go ahead. Say it."

"Say what?"

"You think I'm still a slacker."

"I don't know you well enough to make that judgment."

"I'm sure Dixie shared enough stories about my exploits for you to form an opinion."

"Dixie loves you, Porter. She believes all her brothers walk on water."

"It would be nice if she let us know that instead of complaining about everything we do." He grew quiet for a minute, then said, "One day I'm going to buy a ranch."

"Where?"

"I've got my eye on a place in the Fortuna Foothills."

"That's a nice area." Buying property in the foothills would require a large chunk of money, and she doubted Porter's employment history of hit-or-miss seasonal jobs would convince a bank to give him a loan.

What if Porter was rustling bulls under Buddy's nose and selling them on the black market in order to finance his dream? As soon as the thought entered her mind, she pushed it away.

"So what do you say?" he said.

"What do I say about what?"

"Having a little fun before we pack it in for the night?"

"It's late. I'm not—"

"Ten o'clock isn't late." When she didn't comment, he said, "C'mon. Let your hair down." He nodded to the clip that pinned her hair to her head. "I've never seen you with your hair loose."

"I wear it up because it's cooler and it doesn't get in my way at work."

"If it's a pain then cut it."

Her long, silky hair was her best feature— according to her mother. "I've thought about it, but don't men prefer long hair?" She winced. Porter would assume she was fishing for compliments.

"I can't speak for every guy, but there's more to a girl than her hair and makeup."

That all sounded good but… "If you feel that way, why does Dixie believe you need to raise your standards and date women with brains, not—"

"Boobs?" He laughed. "I have nothing against serious girls, except that most of them don't know how to have fun. All work and no play stinks."

"Are you insinuating that I'm no fun?" she teased, knowing that it was the truth. The last time she'd goofed off with a guy had been in college, when Tyler had taken her to a miniature golf course.

"I'm not insinuating. I'm flat-out saying it's so," he said.

She'd show him she knew how to party. "Go ahead and stop somewhere."

"You sure?"

"Positive."

Two miles later Porter pulled into the parking lot of a bar.

"The place doesn't look busy," Wendy said.

"It's a Monday night. Only the regulars will be here." He got out, then helped Wendy from the cab.

"What's the name of the bar?" she asked.

"The Red Rooster." He pointed to the rooster weather vane on the roof of the building. And the black door sported the silhouette of a red rooster on it.

When they entered the establishment, a wailing soprano voice threatened to wash them back outside. Karaoke night was in full swing and a redhead in pink spandex and a rhinestone tank top belted out Patsy Cline's "Walkin' After Midnight" while a handful of men leered at her through beer-goggle eyes.

Porter grasped Wendy's hand and led her to the bar.

A short man with a grizzled face and a potbelly stepped through a pair of swinging doors behind the bar. He wobbled over and asked, "Where are you folks from?"

"Yuma," Porter said.

"I need to buy me a house down there. Can't take the cold winters up here no more." He slapped drink napkins on the bar. "What can I get you?"

"I'll have a draft—" Wendy poked him in the side. "Make that a Dr Pepper," Porter said.

"Scotch, neat, please." She smiled at Porter's wide-eyed stare. "You expected me to order wine?"

"Or beer. Where'd you learn to drink Scotch?"

"Most of my clients are men."

"I guess there aren't a lot of women running livestock ranches these days," he said.

"There are some, but corporations are taking over the beef industry and family-owned ranches are disappearing."

The barkeep delivered Wendy's Scotch and she nodded to Porter. "He's buying." She tossed down the drink, then set the glass on the bar. "I'll take another." Two drinks would relax her. When the barkeep delivered her refill, her stomach had warmed from the alcohol and her ears no longer winced at the crazy lady singing another oldie but goody. After the second song the rhinestone beauty abandoned the microphone and a quarter found its way into the jukebox.

"Let's dance." Porter held out his hand.

Wendy finished her drink, then stood and swayed toward Porter. She braced her hands against his chest and closed her eyes. "Whoever built this place did a horrible job with the floors. They're sloped downward."

Porter's chuckle drifted into her ear. Wendy could get used to having his hands on her. Standing this close to him, she noticed the bump on the bridge of his nose—he'd probably broken it roughhousing with his brothers. She shifted her gaze to his mouth. How would those masculine lips feel…? He lowered his head, closing the distance between their faces.

No. She pushed away from him and walked over to the stage. She picked up the microphone and tapped her finger against it, then jumped at the loud thump that echoed from the speakers on the floor.

"How does this work?"

Right then the song "Nine to Five" by Dolly Parton began playing and the screen hanging from the ceiling displayed the lyrics. Wendy made an attempt to sing along, but couldn't keep up with the bouncing ball and sounded like an idiot. When the song ended, the group of men whistled. "Would you like me to sing another?" she asked.

"One song is enough," Porter said.

"I wasn't that bad, was I?" She looked at her fans. The men saluted her with their beer bottles.

"How about a game of darts?" Porter asked.

"I've never played before." She accepted his help off the stage.

"I'll show you how to hit the bull's-eye." He laid money on the bar and the barkeep handed them two sets of darts.

"Can I have the blue ones?" she asked.

"Sure." Porter stood behind Wendy, grasped her wrist and raised her arm.

"What are you doing?" she whispered when his breath feathered across the back of her neck.

"Showing you how to throw." He pulled her arm back and then thrust it forward. She released the dart and it sailed across the room, hitting the wall next to the board.

"You're not a very good teacher," she said, turning around.

"I'm better at other things." The heat in his eyes stole her breath.

If you kiss him, you'll compromise your investigation.

Right now she didn't care about her job. All she wanted was to feel Porter's mouth on hers.

He stepped back suddenly. "It's late. We'd better go."

Wendy followed, relieved one of them had come to their senses before it was too late—she just wished it had been her and not Porter.

Chapter Four

Dang. Porter had almost kissed Wendy. Good thing he'd come to his senses before he'd made that blunder.

He held her arm as they crossed the parking lot. Two Scotches had made her tipsy—hopefully tipsy enough that she wouldn't remember their almost kiss. Shoot, he didn't dare do anything to jeopardize his job with Del Mar Rodeo.

Still, he wouldn't be a man if he didn't admit that a part of him wanted Wendy to mull over what almost happened tonight. Why? Because she'd wiggled her way beneath his skin. She was unlike any of the women he'd known or dated. He tended to avoid responsible, career-minded females. But Wendy had loosened up and the sparkle in her brown eyes had triggered a few fantasies—riding horses in the mountains together, taking a walk through the pecan groves, the two of them sitting in the front seat of his truck listening to a Luke Bryan CD.

You could have kissed her inside the bar. She wouldn't have stopped you.

That's exactly why he hadn't kissed her. The joke would have been on him when Wendy rolled out of bed tomorrow and realized she'd made a huge mistake. Then he'd look like a fool. And if being embarrassed wasn't enough motivation to keep his hands and his lips to himself, knowing Dixie would never forgive him if he hurt her friend was.

He opened the passenger-side door, but Wendy didn't get in. "What's the matter?"

She stared him square in the eye. "Why?"

"Why what?"

"Why didn't you kiss me?"

Oh, man. The Wendy glaring at him didn't appear tipsy anymore—maybe the cool evening air had cleared the alcohol fog from her head. Porter worried anything that came out of his mouth would land him in trouble, but her steely stare insisted she wasn't backing down.

"You had too much to drink and I didn't want to take advantage of you." That sounded noble.

"Bull."

His mouth sagged open.

"Don't lie. You didn't kiss me because you're not attracted to me."

"What?" Maybe the bartender had slipped a Mickey into her drink and she was hallucinating.

"I'm not as sexy as those buckle bunnies who cheered for you at the rodeo."

"The heck you aren't."

She cupped her hands around her petite breasts and pushed them together. "My boobs aren't big enough, are they?"

Holy smokes. Someone would have to put a loaded gun to his head before he answered that question.

She fluffed her hair. "And I'm not a blonde."

"I like your dark hair." Especially when she wore it loose and the strands fell across her shoulders.

"I don't have curves."

He put one hand on each hip and his fingertips almost met in the middle of her back. "Your curves are perfect." He wanted to slide his hands beneath her shirt and caress her naked skin.

"Plus, I'm short."

"You're the perfect height." If he pulled her against him, the top of her head would fit snugly beneath his chin. All this talk about her *imperfect* body played havoc with his male anatomy, and his jeans grew uncomfortably tight. "You finished?"

"Finished with what?"

"Your tirade."

She stamped her foot on top of his boot.

"Ouch!" He dropped his hands from her waist.

"I don't know why I ever thought you were cute."

He grinned. "You think I'm cute?"

"I used to back in high school."

Porter recalled one afternoon when Wendy visited the pecan farm and her eyes had followed him when he and his brothers had played football in the yard.

"Now you're nothing but a…a…"

"Go on."

"A…a…womanizer!"

He couldn't deny the charge. He'd flirted with a lot of cowgirls through the years, but what most people didn't know was that he could count on a single hand— minus the thumb and forefinger—the number of one-night stands he'd had. He wasn't a love 'em and leave 'em kind of guy. He liked spending time with a woman and getting to know her. And right now he was thinking he'd really like to get to know Wendy as more than his sister's friend.

"Well, say something!"

"You've had too much to drink."

"And you've got a big ego."

Big ego? He couldn't think of anything he'd done or accomplished that was important enough to brag about. He was nothing better or worse than a down-home country boy. "It's one in the morning and we haven't checked into a motel yet."

"For a guy who enjoys partying, you're in a hurry to end the night."

Porter regretted bullying her into proving she knew how to have fun. If he'd known it would be a touchy subject with her, he never would have suggested they stop for a drink. "Hop in the truck, Wendy."

"Is it true what your sister said? That the reason you date airheads is because you have no self-confidence?"

Ouch.

"Dixie thinks you're afraid of girls with brains because they'll see through you."

The conversation was becoming less and less amusing. "See through me to what?" As soon as he asked the question he wanted to take it back. Arguing with an inebriated woman was not a smart thing to do.

"See that you're intimidated by smart women. Women who have more than big boobs and pretty faces going for them."

He reacted without thinking, grabbing her shoulders and pressing her against the side of the trailer. "Just remember—" his mouth hovered above hers "—I gave you a chance to shut up." Then he kissed her.

Porter expected Wendy to push him away—instead, she curled her arms around his neck and sank into his body. Her mouth was soft and inviting and by his second pass across her lips, he was lost. Needing more, he flicked his tongue against the corner of her mouth, and she opened to him. She tasted like sweet whiskey and he couldn't get enough of her no matter which way he angled his head. When her tongue entered his mouth, he groaned at the electric zap that shot through his chest and headed south to his groin. With her body plastered against him, it was impossible to hide his arousal from her. Only when Wendy's moan drifted into his mouth did he realize he was cupping her breast.

The soft mound fit perfectly in his palm, and he wanted nothing more than to strip off her shirt and bra and see her naked. He moved his hand to the back of her head and held her steady as he deepened the kiss.

The rumble of a car engine reminded him that they were standing outside in plain view, and he ended the kiss slowly…a nibble here. A nibble there. The lights in the parking lot provided enough illumination for him to make out Wendy's expression. *Dazed* was the best word to describe her vacant stare.

"Was that the kiss of a man who's intimidated by a smart, savvy woman?"

Wendy opened her mouth but no words came out and she didn't protest when he set his hands on her waist and lifted her into the truck cab. He shut the door and got in on the driver's side. He was afraid to look at Wendy, because he knew she wouldn't stop him if he tried to kiss her again.

"Porter."

He kept his eyes on the steering wheel. "What?"

"You're a good kisser."

Swallowing a groan, he turned the key in the ignition and shifted gear. The motel wasn't far, but Wendy fell asleep before he'd even driven a mile. When they arrived at the Holiday Inn Express, the parking lot was jammed. He left a snoozing Wendy locked in the cab and went into the motel to register.

"I'm sorry, we only have one room left," the night manager said.

"Okay, I'll check out the Best Western."

"They're full up, too. Hampton Ball Bearing is hosting its national conference this week and the motels in town are all booked. The room I have available was a late cancellation."

The ball-bearing gods were conspiring against Porter. "I'll take the room." He handed over his credit card. "And I need a rollaway."

"I'm afraid all the rollaway beds are in use."

Great. Porter signed on the dotted line, then slid the key cards into his pocket and returned to the truck. "Hey, sleepyhead." He shook Wendy's shoulder. "We're at the motel."

He helped her from the cab, then made sure she was steady on her feet before he grabbed the overnight bags and locked the truck. Their room was on the first floor next to the exit, and he ushered her inside, then locked the door.

"What's wrong?" he asked when she scowled at him.

"Is this my room or yours?"

"We're sharing the room."

"There's only one bed," she said.

"The motel's booked solid. We got the last available room."

She stared at him as if he'd left his brains in the truck. "But there's only one bed."

"I'll sleep on top of the covers."

"Did you ask for a rollaway?"

"They're all in use," he said.

Her gaze swung between him and the bed. She'd snuggled up to him while they shot darts then allowed him to kiss the daylights out of her when they left the bar, but evidently the short nap in the truck cab cleared her alcoholic haze and, like him, she wasn't happy sharing a room.

Without a word, Wendy took her luggage and disappeared into the bathroom.

Porter flipped on the TV, removed his boots and belt, then stretched out across the bed—on top of the covers—and watched Mr. Muscle demonstrate how to use the Bowflex home gym. Two hours later a dull twinge in Porter's neck dragged him out of dreamland and he opened his eyes to a dark room and Wendy's head resting on his chest.

He must have fallen asleep while she'd taken a shower. He was reluctant to move, deciding he liked having her snuggled against his side even if she slept beneath the covers. But his bladder demanded relief so he slid out from under Wendy and went into the bathroom. Twenty minutes later, after he brushed his teeth and took a hot shower, he was wide-awake. Back in the bedroom he sat in the chair and studied Wendy's dark silhouette in bed.

She didn't come close to any of the women he'd dated. She was smart—not that he made a habit of dating dummies, but most of the girls he took out didn't aspire to higher goals than finding a husband, settling down and having children. Nothing wrong with that dream, but he admitted there was something sexy about a woman who was out in the world succeeding in life without a man by her side.

In the end it didn't matter how Wendy impressed him. She wanted to go places with her career and all he wanted to do was stay put on a ranch and raise bucking horses. As much as she'd loosened up tonight and was fun to be with, he expected her to wake in the morning and act as if nothing had happened between them. Even his kiss would be a distant memory.

He and Wendy were a simple case of opposites attracting. He'd be wise to spend his energy doing his job well so he didn't make a mistake and end up in Wendy's report.

PORTER TURNED THE cattle truck onto a dirt path and drove through the gates of the Eagle's Nest Ranch, five miles outside of Grand Junction, Colorado. Wendy exhaled a sigh of relief after enduring the hour-long ride in silence. Porter hadn't spoken a word since leaving the motel. She worried that if either of them began a conversation, the subject would inevitably turn to the night before and her odd behavior. She'd believed a drink or two would magically turn her into a fun person— instead she'd acted like an idiot.

As much as she appreciated not having to analyze her embarrassing behavior, she yearned to know if Porter had enjoyed their kiss as much as she had.

You should never have had that first drink.

She shuddered when she pictured her mother's reaction if she learned her daughter had drunk Scotch in a bar called the Red Rooster, sung karaoke and played darts with a livestock-hauling cowboy. Wendy peeked across the seat at Porter. He stared out the windshield, both hands on the wheel, and concentrated on driving the narrow gravel path. She understood why women were drawn to him—he was easy on the eyes and fun to be with. Even with all the pressures of her job and her boss counting on her to help solve the case of the missing bulls, her stress level decreased in Porter's presence.

When she reflected back on the men her father had set her up with—men with serious drive and lofty career aspirations—she'd never felt at ease in their company even though she'd had a lot more in common with them than with Porter. Wendy wasn't sure what that said about her. For now she'd blame her relaxed state on the lingering effects of Porter's sexy mouth.

"What's so amusing?"

She jumped inside her skin. "Nothing. Why?"

"You were smiling."

She frowned. "Is that better?"

The truck hit a bump, and Porter's gaze swung back to the road.

"What do you know about the Eagle's Nest?" She'd done her research before the trip but was curious to learn if Porter knew any details she hadn't uncovered.

"Only that Buddy's done business with the ranch before."

"The property is close to twenty thousand acres. John Kruger is the ranch manager and he's in charge of everyday operations." He was also responsible for breeding bulls, raising beef cattle and scheduling big-game hunting excursions. Kruger had tried his hand at rodeo after graduating high school but had quit following a series of injuries. He'd returned to his hometown in Montana, where he and his eldest brother had butted heads over how to run the family construction business.

Not long after, he'd left home again and hired on as a ranch hand for the Rimrock Ranch in northern Colorado. Three years into the job he'd been promoted to foreman and married the boss's daughter. A year later they divorced after he'd been caught having an affair with the housemaid. He left Rimrock Ranch and found his way to the Eagle's Nest, where he was eventually promoted to ranch manager.

"Who owns the ranch?" Porter asked.

"A group of East Coast investors." Eight businessmen in all. Wendy had looked into their backgrounds but found nothing unusual about their business dealings. Kruger, on the other hand, was a person of interest, because an insurance claim filed by Buddy had stated that one of his bulls had gone missing after it left Eagle's Nest.

Buildings came into view in the distance—three barns, the main house and smaller sheds along with several pickups dotted the ranch yard. Porter slowed the cattle truck to a crawl and parked next to an empty corral.

Before either of them opened their doors, a large man with a dark handlebar mustache stepped outside of the main house. John Kruger. He wore ranch attire—jeans, a Western shirt, boots and a cowboy hat. The gun strapped to his hip hinted that he meant business.

If Porter thought the weapon was unusual, he didn't say so. He grabbed the clipboard and left the truck. Wendy hurried after him. He stopped at the porch steps and held out his hand. "Porter Cash."

"John Kruger. What happened to Scott?"

"Scott who?" Porter glanced at Wendy.

"Scott Phillips. He transported the bulls for Del Mar Rodeo last time."

Wendy's senses went on alert—apparently Kruger knew nothing about Scott Phillips being fired from Del Mar after the bull he'd picked up from the Eagle's Nest Ranch went missing. Either the ranch manager was playing dumb or he had nothing to do with the missing bull. If he was innocent, then Wendy had to consider the possibility that Buddy Davidson might be setting up his drivers to take the fall for his shenanigans.

Kruger nodded to Wendy. "Who's your partner?"

"Wendy Chin. She's—"

"A girlfriend." Wendy shoved her hand at Kruger, forcing him to shake it. Then she batted her eyelashes and slipped her arm through Porter's, hoping he wouldn't give her away.

Kruger appeared uninterested in her relationship with Porter and said, "The bulls are behind the barn. I'll have one of my men release them into the paddock by the truck. You'll have to back up to the gate on the opposite side." He walked off.

"Friendly fellow," she muttered.

"Girlfriend? What was that all about?"

"I don't want anyone knowing that I work for an insurance company."

"Why not?" Porter headed back to the truck.

Wendy had to take two steps for every one of his. "Because."

"Because why?"

She suspected he knew she was hiding something from him. Her gut insisted Porter had nothing to do with the missing bulls, but if she revealed the truth about why she'd tagged along on the trip, the people involved might become spooked and she'd never find out if Del Mar Rodeo was scamming American Livestock Insurance.

"Can you just trust me on this, Porter?"

He opened the passenger-side door and helped her into the cab then hopped in behind the wheel. "I didn't say anything when we started out yesterday, but I get the feeling this isn't a typical insurance agent ride-along."

Darn him for being perceptive.

"It's not, but I can't tell you anything more."

He started the truck, then backed the trailer to the gate. For a guy who was relatively new at transporting cattle, Porter handled the semi with ease. After he shut off the engine, he said, "So last night was all part of an act?"

"Act?"

"You pretending you don't know how to have fun."

"If you're insinuating I was trying to get information out of you because I suspect you of foul play, then it was pretty stupid of me to tell you not to drink, wasn't it?"

He shoved a hand through his hair. "What about the kiss? Was that part of your job?"

She couldn't tell if he was serious or teasing, and the longer he studied her, the warmer her face grew. "No, the kiss was not part of my job."

His brown eyes glinted. "So you wouldn't be opposed to me kissing you again?"

Knuckles rapped on the window next to her. A scowling cowboy stood outside the truck. She opened her door.

"You ready to load the bulls?" the man asked.

"Yep." Porter walked off with the ranch hand.

Wendy stayed put. Helping corral bulls was not in her job description, and she didn't want to get in the way and cause one of the animals to charge Porter or the ranch hand.

It took thirty minutes to load five bulls—one stubborn cuss refused to walk up the ramp and the ranch hand swatted his cowboy hat against its rump until the animal finally trotted into the trailer. Once Porter secured the door, he handed the clipboard to the cowboy, who took it into the barn, presumably to get Kruger's signature, then he returned it to Porter and disappeared.

When Porter got into the truck cab, he wore a puzzled frown.

"What's the matter?" she asked.

"I'm tired of people treating me like I don't know what I'm doing." He started the truck. "Kruger told the ranch hand to remind me to stop at Bell Farms to let the cattle rest overnight before continuing to the fairgrounds outside King City tomorrow. I already knew that."

"Maybe he's worried about the animals," she said.

"A ranch hand named Big Sam is supposed to handle the arrangements at Bell Farms, but the paperwork—" Porter nodded to the clipboard "—says Jack Edmonton is the foreman."

"Where is Bell Farms?"

"Near Las Vegas. About seven hours from here."

"Do the bulls have water and feed inside the truck?"

"Water. They were eating in the holding pen all morning, so they'll be fine until we unload them."

One of the animals kicked the side of the trailer, and Porter said, "We'd better get going before they become restless."

As he drove away from the ranch, he slipped a CD into the player. "You like Porter Wagoner?"

"I guess it's only natural that you'd be partial to your namesake's music."

He grinned.

"I don't listen to much country-and-western music."

"What do you listen to?"

"The insurance office plays elevator music."

He stared at her mouth. "Here's a Porter Wagoner classic. 'Misery Loves Company.'"

Chapter Five

"I'm fine, Mom." Wendy lowered her voice. "Yes, I'm eating and yes, I'm getting plenty of rest."

Porter eavesdropped on Wendy's call while he waited for the ranch hand at Bell Farms to tell him where to unload the bulls. After they'd arrived, Wendy had excused herself to make a phone call. He'd assumed she needed to report in to her boss and was surprised that she'd phoned her mother. Who'd have believed a twenty-six-year-old woman had to report in to her mother? Then again, his mother had been AWOL most of his life, so maybe it wasn't odd.

A movement out of the corner of his eye caught his attention. An older cowboy walked out of the barn with a lady by his side. *Holy smokes.* He watched the blonde head his way. She was no buckle bunny but a bona fide cowgirl. She wore fringed chaps, a Western shirt, leather gloves and a hat with a sweat-stained band. Her boots were covered in dirt and manure and there wasn't a rhinestone or bobble of bling anywhere on her. As she drew closer, he saw wrinkles fanning from the corners of her eyes and deep lines bracketing her mouth. Her youth had passed her by years ago, and the sun had turned her skin to leather, but there were hints that she'd once been a looker.

"Ma'am." He tipped his hat. "I've got five Del Mar Rodeo bulls that need an overnight rest." He nodded to the man. "I was told Big Sam would handle the arrangements."

"That's me." The cowpoke removed his work glove and shook Porter's hand. Big Sam was bow-legged and short.

"Margaret Sterns," the woman said. "I'm the new manager of Bell Farms. Sorry about the wait. I wasn't aware until just now that we were keeping your bulls overnight."

"Do you have room for them or do I need to make other arrangements?" Porter asked.

"What's the matter?" Wendy joined the group.

"This is Ms. Sterns. She runs Bell Farms." Porter nodded to Wendy. "Wendy Chin is my copilot on this run."

"I'm afraid there's been a miscommunication," Ms. Sterns said. "No one informed me that we were keeping your bulls."

"I've got the paperwork right here." Porter retrieved the clipboard from the cab and handed over the information.

Ms. Sterns skimmed the contract, her brow furrowing. "Like I thought, this deal was negotiated with Jack Edmonton, and he no longer works here."

Great. Why hadn't Hank doubled-checked the arrangements before Porter had left town?

"I'll allow the bulls to remain overnight, but Del Mar Rodeo will have to find another ranch to board their roughstock."

"Which pen should I unload them in?" Porter asked.

"They can use the corral a mile south of the property."

"Is there water and feed out there for them?"

"I'll have Sam—" she nodded to the cowboy "—deliver hay and water within the hour."

"Ms. Sterns," Sam said, "that pen isn't strong enough to keep a bull in if something spooks it. They'd be safer in the corral next to the barn."

Margaret Sterns stared long and hard at Sam, and Porter got the feeling the woman didn't trust the cowboy. "Fine. Leave them here."

Porter nodded to the clipboard in her hand. "I need your signature. Del Mar Rodeo paid for the feed and space in advance of us arriving." Whether Bell Farms received the check or Jack Edmonton took off with it was anyone's guess.

Margaret signed her name then walked away.

"Give me a minute to get the corral ready," Big Sam said.

While they waited to unload the bulls, Porter returned the clipboard to the cab and phoned his supervisor. "Hank, it's Porter."

"You make it to Bell Farms?"

"Yeah, but the ranch manager wasn't aware of our arrangement."

"I phoned Jack Edmonton over two months ago to verify the details."

"Edmonton was fired, and a new manager named Margaret Sterns has taken over."

Dead air greeted Porter's statement. "Hank, you still there?"

"Yeah. Is Big Sam working at the ranch?"

"Yep."

"You deal with Big Sam. He'll make sure the bulls are fed and watered."

"Sure."

"Porter."

"What?"

"Oh, forget it. It's nothing." The line went dead.

Porter slid behind the wheel and fired up the engine before he realized Wendy wasn't in the cab. He checked his mirrors and spotted her walking with Big Sam. What was she up to now?

He moved the rig to the corral by the barn and waited for Big Sam to signal him to unload. The bulls kicked the sides of the trailer—they wanted out and he didn't blame them. Big Sam gave the thumbs-up after making sure the gate on the other side of the corral was secured. Porter unlatched the trailer door and lowered the ramp.

One by one he coaxed the bulls down the ramp and into the pen. When all five were free, he locked the gate, then stowed the ramp. He noticed Wendy chatting with Big Sam by the corral as the ranch hand slipped a hose between the rails of the pen and filled the water trough. Sam must have cracked a joke because Wendy laughed out loud.

She hadn't guffawed like that since their trip began, and Porter wished he'd been the one to make her laugh. The weird yearning in his gut alarmed him. No matter that the kiss they'd shared the evening before had been off-the-charts amazing, Porter wanted something solid, deeper and long lasting with a woman. And that was the problem—Wendy wasn't a woman a man had a fling with. She was exactly the kind of woman he was looking to go the distance with.

Porter closed in on the pair. "You ready?" He looked at Wendy.

"Ready for what?"

"To find a room and grab something to eat."

"There's a Holiday Inn Express two miles up the highway," Sam said.

"Thanks for the recommendation." Wendy held out her hand. "Nice meeting you. Take good care of our bulls."

"Yes, ma'am." The cowboy tipped his hat, then retreated into the barn.

Porter and Wendy returned to the truck and he flipped on the radio. "What are you hungry for?"

She waved a hand in front of her face. "Anything. You choose."

"I asked you first."

"And I said it doesn't matter."

"You're an unusual woman."

"What's that supposed to mean?"

"The females I know have strong opinions on what kind of food they want to eat." His brothers would never admit it, but their wives ruled the roost. Porter had walked into the farmhouse more than once and caught Conway cooking at the stove with a feather duster sticking out of his back pocket.

"Food is food," Wendy said.

Nothing he liked better than a challenge. "Let's see if there's a Chinese restaurant in town."

She snorted. "Are you trying to be funny?"

He struggled not to laugh. "You're Chinese. Why wouldn't I assume you like Chinese food?"

"I'm an American who enjoys Chinese food." He opened his mouth to speak but she cut him off. "But seeing how I was born and raised in the southwest, I've developed a fondness for Mexican food."

"Okay. Mexican it is." On the outskirts of Grand Junction, he pulled into a convenience store parking lot. "Wait here."

Five minutes later he was back behind the wheel and merging into traffic. He drove a half mile, then veered left toward an adobe ranch house. "The clerk at the store said this place is a favorite with the locals."

"Doesn't look very busy," Wendy said.

All the parking places were empty. "Guess we'll just have to find out for ourselves." He helped Wendy to the ground, then rang the bell when they reached the front door. A young girl, maybe twelve or thirteen, greeted them in Spanish. Porter opened his mouth to tell the kid he didn't speak Spanish, but Wendy rolled off several sentences in the language before he could say anything.

"They don't open for dinner until five," Wendy said. "But her mother will make an exception for us, because we're passing through town."

They followed the girl to a patio off the back of the café, where tables sat in the yard beneath yellow and blue umbrellas. After they were seated, their waitress returned with a basket of homemade tortilla chips and salsa, then spoke to Wendy.

"Maria would like to know what you want to drink," Wendy said.

"Water's fine."

After Wendy gave their drink orders, she sampled the salsa. "This is amazing."

Miffed, he asked, "What else don't I know about you?"

"What do you mean?"

"We've both lived close to the border our whole lives. You speak fluent Spanish and I know only a few words."

"My parents pushed me to learn the language so I could help them with their business. I studied Spanish in high school and minored in the language in college."

Maria delivered glasses of water to the table and spoke to Wendy again.

"We have a choice of chicken tacos or cheese enchiladas," Wendy said.

"I'll take the chicken tacos," Porter said. Wendy ordered the same. When Maria left them alone, he asked, "Do you speak Chinese?"

She shook her head. "Only a few phrases."

Porter squirmed in his seat. Wendy was a bright girl—more intelligent than she led on. *And you're nothing but a livestock hauler and wannabe rancher.* "Why aren't you married?" he asked.

Instead of answering his question, she turned the tables on him. "All your siblings have tied the knot. What's holding you back?"

Heck, there were five girls he could think of off the top of his head who would have said yes if he'd proposed to them.

So why didn't you ask one of them to marry you? Because he hadn't been ready to settle down. "I haven't found the right woman yet."

"My parents would love me to get married. The sooner the better," Wendy said. "But we have a slight difference of opinion on what kind of man is best for me."

"Best for you?"

"You'd have to be Chinese to understand."

"Try me," he said.

Their meals arrived and after Maria left them alone to eat, Porter pushed the subject. "Why do I have to be Chinese to understand?"

"You're a lot like Dixie, you know that?"

"Everyone in the family thinks my sister and Johnny have more in common, since they share the same father."

"Dixie is as stubborn as you are." Wendy toyed with her rice and expelled a long breath. "My parents want me to marry a Chinese man not so much because of our ethnicity, but because they believe Chinese men are dependable, career driven and hardworking. My father is always setting me up on dates with the sons of his business partners."

"But there are other men with those same qualities." A group Porter had consciously excluded himself from—until lately.

"Try telling my father that. Life would be much simpler if I'd been born a boy."

"I've heard stories about Chinese couples valuing sons more than daughters, but I can't believe your parents regret having you." He toasted her with his water glass. "Look at you. You're successful, educated, fluent in two languages and you love Mexican food." He grinned. "You're darn near perfect."

Wendy laughed, and he savored the happy sound. "So was I wrong?"

"Wrong about what?"

"Do you believe your parents regret you were born a girl?"

He was the first person who'd asked Wendy that question. She was certain that a few of her friends and teachers had been curious, but no one had ever broached the subject with her. If Porter had the guts to ask, then he deserved an answer.

"My parents love me and they'll never admit they wanted a son, but I know that's why they've pushed me so hard to succeed at everything I do."

"Aside from all the dedication and hard work, maybe they also want you to marry a Chinese man so they'll finally get the son they'd wished for."

Porter was more perceptive than she gave him credit for.

"I understand now why you were valedictorian of your high school class. You didn't really have a choice, did you?"

"A lot was expected of me." *A lot* had never been enough for her parents. They'd insisted she major in business at ASU even though Wendy had wanted to be a schoolteacher. Her parents believed she'd make more money in business—they valued financial security above all else. When Wendy got the job with American Livestock Insurance, she'd viewed the position as temporary until something more interesting came along. But she'd been raised to go above and beyond in everything she did and within a year she'd earned her first promotion. After the bump in pay she'd thought her parents would back off, but they hadn't. They wouldn't be happy until she became CEO of American Livestock Insurance.

"Okay, so you don't want to marry a man your parents pick for you. Then don't."

"Good advice." She drained her water glass. It was useless to try and explain her parents to Porter—not when their beliefs and value system could be traced back to Confucius.

Wendy wished she had the strength to defy her parents and marry the man of her dreams—whoever he ended up being. If she had to marry a Chinese man, then her parents would have to wait right along with her until she found one who made her heart go pitter-patter.

"How many men has your father set you up with?" Porter asked.

"I lost count after twelve in the past two years." The men she'd dated had been too much like her. "What about you? Have you ever proposed to a girl?"

"Nope."

His curt response surprised Wendy, and she got the feeling that maybe he'd come close to popping the question. Then again maybe not. Guys like Porter—the ones who lived in the moment—never thought about the future.

But they sure know how to have fun.

They finished their meals and declined dessert, so Maria dropped off the check. Wendy snatched it up before Porter could. "My treat."

"You sure?" he asked.

Wendy laughed as she dug through her purse for her credit card.

"What's so funny?"

"You wouldn't understand." The men she'd dated would have been appalled that Porter had acquiesced so quickly when she'd offered to pick up the tab. But Wendy wasn't upset in the least. She appreciated that Porter respected her enough to allow her to pay the bill. If only she could find a man her parents approved of with Porter's personality.

PORTER PARKED THE cattle truck in the lot behind the Holiday Inn Express and cut the engine.

"Aren't you getting a room, too?" Wendy asked when he made no move to get out.

"I'm sleeping in the cab tonight."

"But you got a room last night," she said.

"Because I wanted to make sure you were okay."

Wendy rolled her eyes. "I had two drinks. I wasn't drunk."

True, but he'd wanted to be there in case she'd wandered down the hall to the ice machine then lost her way back to the room and ended up somewhere she shouldn't be.

When she frowned, he explained, "Del Mar gives me an allowance. Whatever I don't spend on the road is added to my paycheck." Porter opted to crash in his truck whenever he could and sock away the extra cash. He hoped that within a year he'd have enough money saved to secure a loan to buy the ranch in Fortuna Foothills. Sleeping on the bench seat was a small price to pay for having goofed off most of his life and blown all the income he'd earned.

"You paid for the motel room the other night."

"It's no big deal," he said.

She pulled her wallet from her purse. "I want to reimburse you."

"I said it was—"

"I know what you said, but my boss covers the cost of my motel rooms and meals." She shoved four twenty-dollar bills at him. "Take it."

He wanted that money more than Wendy would ever know, but he had his pride. "Get yourself a room while I run an errand. I'll be back later."

"I'm not in any rush to settle in," she said. "I'll go with you on your errand."

He didn't want to take Wendy to another dive bar. "Thanks, but I'd rather go alone."

Her eyes widened, and he knew she believed he was going to meet up with a woman or go looking for one.

"When do we leave in the morning?" she asked.

"No later than seven."

"I'll be ready."

She removed her bag from behind the seat, then shut the door. She looked over her shoulder twice before disappearing inside the motel.

He'd hurt her feelings, but he couldn't admit the real reason he didn't want her along with him—he needed a break from her and that sexy perfume she wore that made him dream about doing things with her that he had no business doing.

Porter drove a quarter mile before pulling off at Dave's Sports Bar and Grill. Inside, he ordered a soft drink and munched on peanuts while he watched the Diamondbacks baseball team play the Marlins. The game had just begun and he figured by the time it ended, he'd be too tired to care that he had to spend the night in a truck cab.

By 10:00 p.m. the bar had emptied out and Porter went into the washroom and took a quick sponge bath, then dunked his head beneath the faucet and rinsed his hair. He dried off with paper towels, left a tip on the bar and walked out. When he returned to the motel, he parked the rig at the back of the lot, then dug through his duffel for his toothbrush and a water bottle. Once he'd cleaned his teeth, he punched his travel pillow into shape and placed it against the window before stretching out and propping his boot heels on the passenger-side dashboard. He squirmed into a semicomfortable position, then tipped his cowboy hat over his face and closed his eyes.

Porter had been sleeping less than an hour when a knock on the window startled him awake. He popped into a sitting position and winced as a sharp pain shot through his neck. When his eyes focused he saw Wendy standing next to the truck. He opened the door.

"What are you doing outside dressed in…?" He nodded to her silky shorts and tank top. The breeze kicked up and plastered the floral print to her petite breasts, leaving little to his imagination. "You look cold. Go back inside." *Please.*

"I can't sleep knowing you're out here. We have a long day tomorrow and I don't want you dozing off at the wheel. You'll rest better in my room."

Was she joking? "I was sleeping just fine until you woke me up."

"Don't be stubborn. Get out of the truck."

"No." *Damn.* He sounded like an ill-tempered child.

A pickup pulled into the lot, its headlights sweeping across Wendy's half-naked body. Enough was enough. Porter grabbed his bag and hopped out of the cab. Taking her by the arm, he escorted her into the motel. Once they were in her room, he said, "You go outside in skimpy clothes like those—" he motioned to her outfit "—and you can expect a drunken cowboy to come knocking on your door."

She went up on tiptoe, pressed her nose against his neck and sniffed. "I don't smell any perfume. Couldn't find any bimbos to hook up with?"

He shut his eyes and squeezed his hands into fists to keep from pulling her closer.

"Is it me?" she asked.

"Is it you, what?" His voice sounded hoarse.

"Am I the real reason you didn't get a motel room tonight?"

"I told you I'm saving the money..."

She licked her lips, and Porter's attention zeroed in on the trail of moisture left behind by her tongue.

"Did I give you the impression that I was interested in—" she stood on tiptoe, bringing her mouth closer to his "—this?" The word floated across his face a second before he felt her mouth press against his.

A white flag shot up in the back of Porter's mind. He was done resisting whatever was happening between him and Wendy. She might be his sister's friend and they might have little in common, but she was a grown woman capable of taking care of herself and making her own decisions. Who was he to turn down an invite into her bed? But gallantry dictated that he offer her one last chance to change her mind.

"Are you sure?" he asked.

Wendy kissed him, and that was as good as yes in his book.

Chapter Six

This was crazy.

Insane.

Foolish.

And the most titillating, exciting, thrilling risk Wendy had ever taken. She could barely think straight with Porter's mouth nibbling her neck as he walked her across the room to the bed. He followed her down to the mattress, kissing a path along her collarbone.

Tiny pulses of electricity coursed through her body as she tugged his shirt from his jeans. When she fumbled with his belt, he trapped her hand against his buckle. "In a hurry, darlin'?"

"God, yes." Was he crazy? She hadn't had sex in… good grief, at least a year and a half.

Had it been that long?

Wendy squirmed against Porter and breathed in his warm male scent. He smelled so good she wanted to taste him—all of him. She attempted to move her mouth to his throat but he covered her lips with his, swallowing her gasp. She'd never been this excited or turned on before. Why Porter? Was it a simple case of opposites attracting, or was she drawn to him because she knew she could never be with him?

Or maybe he makes you believe you're strong enough to stand up to your own parents and fight for what you want—what makes you happy.

She shut out the voice in her head and focused on the feel of Porter's fingers sifting through her hair and his lips teasing her mouth. Now that her hands were free, she worked the buckle open and unzipped his jeans. She slid her fingers inside his BVDs and found him rock hard. He groaned in her ear, and she shivered.

Her power to arouse him emboldened her, and she pushed him onto his back and straddled his hips. Then she pulled off her pajama top and the warm gleam in his eyes sent her pulse racing. He reached for her breasts, caressing first one then the other before he teased and tormented them with his mouth.

She'd never had sex like this—with the lights on. And she'd never felt so uninhibited and wild.

Porter's fingers eased inside her silk pajama shorts and worked their magic until she exploded, shattering into a million shards of brilliant white light. Head spinning, she collapsed on top of his chest. Before she caught her breath, he switched their positions and pushed her shorts down her legs.

"That's better." He popped off the bed—hair rumpled from her fingers, mouth red from their kisses—and removed his clothes, offering Wendy a full-frontal view of his cowboy awesomeness.

"You're… *Wow.*"

"Wait until I show you my moves." He pounced, sprawling across her. Then he gazed into her eyes, and Wendy worried he would see into her soul. See how she desperately wished she was someone other than Wendy Chin. She attempted to look away, but he caressed her jaw and gazed into her eyes. His intimate stare was sexy and arousing—was there anything about him that wasn't sexy? He traced her lips with his tongue, then deepened the kiss.

A voice in her head warned her that making love with Porter was dangerous. He tempted her to forget her place in the world…what was expected of her. In Porter's arms she didn't care about duty, responsibility or pleasing her parents. She only cared about the way his touch sent her blood roaring through her ears.

The caresses grew in intensity, and Wendy gave herself over to his experienced hands. It wasn't long before the sheets became twisted and rumpled beneath their tangle of arms and legs.

"Are you ready?" Her body answered the husky question with an involuntary shiver.

Porter reached for his jeans on the floor. After he sheathed himself, he kissed her gently, slowly, deeply as he entered her. She gave herself over to his expertise and soared with him to their own little sliver of heaven.

WHAT THE HECK *had happened?*

It was four-thirty in the morning. Porter lay with Wendy's warm, naked body plastered against him and every light in the room blazing. He stared at the popcorn ceiling and took shallow, even breaths so he wouldn't wake the sex kitten in his arms.

Who would have believed Wendy Chin—Ms. Brainiac, Ms. Career Woman, Ms. Valedictorian, Ms. Perfect—would morph into a red-hot chili pepper in bed? He couldn't recall one girl he'd slept with who'd set him on fire the way she had.

What did it all mean?

Relax. It was just sex between two consenting adults.

If someone had told him a few months ago that he'd be hauling bulls to rodeos and sleeping with his sister's friend, he would have called them crazy. Maybe he was making a bigger deal of it than he needed to. The sex was amazing, but why him? Why had serious Wendy picked his bones to jump?

Don't tell your boss that I'm riding along with you.

Since the start of the trip he'd battled a nagging suspicion that Wendy's company was more involved than she claimed. He closed his eyes, and a vision of Veronica Patriot popped into his head. He didn't want to believe Wendy had made love to him in hopes that their closeness would encourage him to reveal secret information about the missing bulls. Information he didn't have.

Wendy's not like Veronica.

That was the truth. She was different from the vindictive buckle bunny in every way. But Porter worried that her dedication to her job and her need to succeed might have fueled her decision to sleep with him. With his mind in turmoil and his body ready to go another round with Wendy, coming up with a decent morning-after line would be nothing short of a challenge.

"I'LL WAIT FOR you in the truck." Porter grabbed his duffel and left the motel room.

As far as morning-after lines, Wendy decided that Porter's took first place in the cuts-like-a-knife category. She peeked around the curtain and watched him stroll to the end of the parking lot where the livestock trailer sat. Last night had been amazing. Porter had shown her more moves in bed than a professional bull rider. And to top it off, she'd woken up this morning feeling restless.

She wouldn't consider herself *experienced* in the art of lovemaking, but she wasn't a novice, either. Sex with Porter had left her yearning for more. More of something that had nothing to do with sex.

Get over it.

She moved away from the window and finished packing. As much as she'd enjoyed spending the night in Porter's arms, she didn't want to leave him with the impression that she expected them to sleep together for the duration of the trip. Last night had been a onetime thing, but the connection she'd felt with Porter made her wish that a motel bed wasn't the only place they were compatible.

Her gaze landed on the mattress, triggering an X-rated flashback. She'd never forget last night. When she was old and frail she'd take the memory out of storage, dust it off and then spend hours imagining what her life would have been like with Porter by her side.

Fairy tales weren't meant for women like Wendy. Reality dictated that she focus on finding an acceptable man her parents would approve of.

You're hiding behind your parents because you're afraid of loving again.

Wendy hated it when her conscience picked on her. She admitted that Tyler's betrayal had cut deep and left her scarred. Even if the right man came along and captured her heart, she wasn't sure she could trust herself to take a chance on him. As much as she hated the idea, it was safer if her parents picked a man for her— that way she wouldn't have to worry about her heart getting broken.

She swung her bag over her shoulder and left the room. When she reached the truck, Porter avoided eye contact with her. He didn't wait for her to secure her seat belt before shifting into gear and pulling out of the lot. The tension in the cab grew thicker by the second. When they stopped at the first traffic light, she said, "I'm hungry. Why don't we pick up breakfast at a drive-through?"

"Sure." His clipped response stung. She guessed he was concerned she'd make a stink about having sex but in all honesty, it had been nothing more than a fling.

Wanting to put him at ease, she said, "About last night—"

"Yeah, about that." His gaze connected with hers. "No big deal."

Blast him—she'd wanted to be the one to say it was no big deal. "Agreed."

"You're okay?" he asked.

"Sure. Are you okay?"

His knuckles whitened against the wheel and he expelled a harsh breath. "Of course I'm okay."

"What's that supposed to mean?" She mimicked his loud huff. All she'd wanted was for him to know he was off the hook and that she didn't expect anything from him. When he didn't respond to her, she said, "We'll forget it ever happened." She stared out the window and willed herself not to cry. They both knew they weren't compatible, so why was she upset that he seemed okay, if not relieved, there wouldn't be a repeat of last night?

Because you don't really feel that way.

She cursed the voice in her head and told herself that she was miffed about spending the night in Porter's arms because the experience had opened her eyes

to all she'd miss if she settled for a man her parents selected for her—a man she didn't love.

You don't love Porter.

Of course she didn't. But she liked Porter. A lot. And
so what if after one night in his arms he'd earned a place
on her keeper shelf of favorite memories?

Porter pulled into a fast-food parking lot and stopped.
"I'll stay with the truck if you want to run in and grab
us breakfast." He removed his wallet from his pocket.

"What would you like?" she asked.

"Two breakfast burritos and a coffee."

She ignored the ten-dollar bill he held out and hopped
down from the cab. If she slammed the door too hard it
was because the handle had slipped from her fingers.
Fifteen minutes later she returned with their food, and
Porter wolfed down his meal, then merged with traffic.

Wendy picked at her hash browns. Thankfully they
were halfway through the trip. Once they reached the
fairgrounds and delivered the bulls, they could go their
separate ways until the end of the day.

"Busy place," Porter said when they arrived at Bell
Farms. There were several pickups parked by the barn
and two of the three pens were filled with horses.

"I don't see the bulls," Wendy said.

"They must have moved the animals to make room
for the horses." He cut the engine. "There's Big Sam.
Let's ask him." They met the ranch hand in front of
the round pen.

"Where are the bulls?" Porter asked.

"Behind the barn," Big Sam said. "Bring the truck
back there."

Wendy waited with Big Sam while Porter positioned
the trailer next to the pen, then opened the back doors

and lowered the ramp. When she noticed Porter had left the clipboard in the truck, she retrieved it from the cab. Each bull had an identification number stamped on his hide and she wanted to verify their IDs as they loaded.

Big Sam disappeared inside the barn, then returned with an armful of fresh alfalfa. The bulls caught the scent of food and followed the ranch hand across the pen. When Big Sam reached the loading ramp, he tossed the remainder of the alfalfa inside the trailer and the bulls followed the scent to where Porter waited to secure them in their individual stalls.

Wendy glanced at each animal's number, making sure they matched up with the paperwork. "Hold on," she said. Wendy hadn't paid close attention when they'd picked up the bulls at Eagle's Nest Ranch, but she'd thought the five animals were colored black-and-white. She couldn't recall a bull with a red hue.

"What's the matter?" Porter jumped to the ground next to her.

"I don't think the red one is ours."

"His number's 723."

She shook her head. "There is no 723 on this list."

"This one giving you trouble?" Big Sam appeared at Porter's side.

"The numbers don't match up," Porter said. "This bull isn't ours."

"You must be mistaken." Big Sam held his hand out to Wendy, and she gave him the clipboard.

"The bull we're missing is 826," she said.

The ranch hand's mouth tightened as he handed her the clipboard. "Maybe they typed the number wrong."

"Did you mix the Del Mar bulls with other rough-stock overnight?" Porter asked.

While the men talked, Wendy walked off to do a little investigating of her own. All was quiet when she entered the barn, and she noticed that the stalls were empty. She turned to leave but a thumping sound caught her attention. She moved farther into the building and poked her head through a doorway in the back, where she discovered a bull eating grain from a bucket. She flipped on the light switch.

Well, well, well.

"Hello, 826." Wendy spun on her boot heels and returned to the pen, Porter and Big Sam still debated over the unfamiliar bull.

"I found him," she said. The men stopped arguing and stared. She nodded to the barn. "He's in the storeroom." She jutted her chin when Big Sam leveled a mean glare at her.

"Wait here."

Once the ranch hand was out of earshot, she asked Porter, "Has this ever happened before?"

"Not on any of my runs."

Big Sam led the bull from the barn and released him into the pen then coaxed 723 into an adjoining pen. Porter left plenty of room between him and 826 as he guided the animal into the trailer. Once the bull was loaded, Porter stowed the ramp and locked the door.

Big Sam was nowhere to be found.

"Wait here." Porter cut across the gravel drive and skipped up the steps to the main house. He pounded on the front door. Margaret Sterns answered, and Wendy wished she could eavesdrop on the conversation.

When Porter returned to the truck, he said, "Let's head out." It wasn't until they reached the highway that he spoke again. "Margaret will probably fire Big Sam."

"She should. Don't you find it curious that one of the bulls had been kept apart from the group?"

"Not necessarily. Some bulls do fine being confined with others and some don't. If a bull becomes antsy or aggressive, the ranch hand will move it somewhere else. What isn't normal is for a ranch hand to be so careless or forgetful that he brings out the wrong bull."

Careless and forgetful was too generous. Wendy wondered if Big Sam was in cahoots with Buddy Davidson to scam American Livestock Insurance. One thing that was becoming clearer was that Porter most likely had nothing to do with the missing bulls. If he was guilty of anything, it was not paying attention to details. After today's snafu, she was certain he'd check and double-check the ID of each bull when they were loaded and unloaded. "How long until we reach King City?"

"Six hours."

Six hours was an eternity to keep her mind from straying to Porter and what they did last night, especially when he sat twelve inches away from her. Resigning herself to a long day of awkwardness, she opened her iPad. Maybe work would help time pass quickly.

Somehow she doubted that.

PORTER FUMED. WHAT the heck had Big Sam tried to pull at Bell Farms? The ranch hand had made a fool out of him in front of Wendy. He might not have checked the bulls' numbers as they loaded, but he knew them by sight. He would have noticed the unfamiliar bull, but Wendy had beaten him to the punch. And that bothered the crap out of him. Since the start of the trip, she'd been watching his every move.

The last thing Porter wanted was to get fired. He needed this job.

After this rodeo, Porter had been instructed to deliver the bulls to a ranch near King City, where the animals would spend a month resting before competing in another rodeo. Once he handed over the bulls he'd be off the hook if any of them mysteriously disappeared.

Now if only he felt as though he was off the hook for last night. He glanced across the seat at Wendy, typing away on her iPad. They were approximately the same age and even though he believed she worked too hard, she had her life in order—unlike him.

Last night she didn't work too hard.

His face warmed at the memory. He'd had more fun than he'd had in a long while. He'd seen a whole new side of Wendy and for a short time had forgotten how wrong they were for each other. Today she reminded him that she was smart as a whip and nothing slipped past her.

He wanted to tell her how much he enjoyed being with her, but feared she'd get the wrong idea and assume he was angling for another invitation into her bed.

But you are...angling.

Okay, so he did want to sleep with Wendy again, but that didn't mean he'd cave in to those urges. It had rubbed him raw this morning that she'd acted as if what they'd shared hadn't been special. "Is it because Dixie's your friend?" Oh, man. Did he just blurt that out loud?

Wendy looked up from the computer screen. "Is what because Dixie and I are friends?"

"Nothing." He had a habit of talking out loud to himself when he was on the road.

"If you're worried I'll tell Dixie we slept together…I hadn't planned on sharing that with her."

"I wasn't worried."

"You don't intend to tell her, do you?" she asked.

"No."

"Good. No sense telling anyone."

Porter winced.

"How long did you say until we arrive in King City?"

Wendy must be feeling the need to escape, too. "Six hours." *Six long hours.*

Porter's phone rang, and he glanced at the name that appeared on the screen. *Hank.* He didn't feel like talking to his boss, so he let the call go to his voice mail.

Apparently Wendy had no problem conducting her business in front of him. She pulled out her phone and made a call. "Mr. McCoy, this is Wendy Chin from American Livestock Insurance. How are you?"

Porter attempted to ignore the conversation, but it was difficult. Wendy assured Mr. McCoy that his rates wouldn't increase if he added fifty head to his herd. She answered several questions, then closed the call with "It was a pleasure talking to you, Mr. McCoy. Give Helen my best."

"You're good," Porter said.

"I'm sorry?"

"You've got a knack for reassuring people."

"Thanks."

Now if only she'd reassure him that what they'd done last night wouldn't come back to kick him in the butt.

Chapter Seven

When Porter pulled into the entrance marked Livestock behind the King City Fairgrounds, Wendy closed her iPad. "Where do you unload the bulls after animal welfare employees okay the paperwork?" she asked.

Porter pointed to a white building with a bull's head painted on the side. "The pens are behind that barn." He stopped at a checkpoint and lowered his window.

"Howdy." A tall, thin man stepped up to the truck.

"I've got five bulls from Del Mar Rodeo Productions." Porter handed over the paperwork.

Wendy listened to the exchange.

"Any problems with the stock during transport?"

"No, sir."

"Have they been let out of the trailer since you left Bell Farms?"

"No."

"How long have they been confined?"

Porter checked his watch. "Six hours and twenty-five minutes."

"Unload them in pen number three so they can be examined before they're put with the other bulls." He handed Porter the documents. "You can park the cattle truck in lot D."

"Thank you." Porter raised the window.

"Do they do this at every rodeo?" Wendy asked.

"If you mean quarantine the bulls when they arrive, yes and no. The smaller rodeos don't bother because they use local livestock, but the bigger rodeos follow different rules."

"Has anything ever happened to one of the animals during transport?"

"Not on my watch." He backed the trailer up to the pen.

Wendy hopped out of the cab and observed. As the animals were unloaded, Porter cross-checked their numbers with the paperwork. Fresh water and feed had been placed inside the pen and the bulls appeared happy with their accommodations.

"You want to stay here while I park the truck?" Porter asked.

"Sure." Left by herself, Wendy studied each bull, checking herself to see that the numbers on their rumps matched with the ones she'd memorized.

"Fine-looking group." An older gentleman approached Wendy, his face a map of wrinkles.

"They certainly are," she said.

He propped a cowboy boot on the lower rung of the corral. "I trust the drive from Grand Junction was uneventful." He smiled, and the crevices in his cheeks deepened.

"How did you know where the bulls came from?" Or that she'd been along for the ride?

He nodded to the building behind him. "There's a lot of tradition here. The fairground dates back to 1910."

Wendy might not know much about how rodeos were

run, but she knew when someone was changing the subject. "I'm sorry, I didn't get your name."

"Looks like the driver's on his way back." He tipped his hat to Wendy. "You enjoy the rodeo, ma'am."

"Who was that?" Porter asked when he stopped at Wendy's side.

"I have no idea." With every passing hour Wendy was more convinced that Porter had nothing to do with the missing Del Mar bulls. She wished she could come clean with him and tell him that her boss suspected Buddy was involved in an insurance fraud scheme. But she didn't want Porter jumping to the conclusion that she'd only slept with him because she hoped he'd reveal information that would incriminate his boss. That was the furthest thing from the truth.

For now she'd keep quiet because her feelings for Porter were a mess. Sleeping with him was the worst best thing she'd ever done. If she was smart, she'd quit analyzing her actions and chalk up the experience to curiosity and a surge of feminine hormones.

"C'mon," Porter said. "I'll show you around, then we'll visit the mom-and-pop diner in town."

"Are we coming back to check on the bulls?" she asked.

"No. Once I deliver them to the fairgrounds my responsibility is finished until I load them up again and drive away."

As they meandered through the crowd, she asked, "How are we getting to this diner?"

Porter pulled a set of keys from his pocket. "A friend loaned me his truck."

She should have guessed he'd run into his buddies

on the circuit. They'd almost made it through the bull barn when a group of cowboys hollered at them.

"If it ain't Porter Wagoner," one of the men called out.

Porter grasped Wendy's fingers and tugged her along. "Hey, Brock. Good to see you." He shook hands with the man, then nodded to the other cowboys and introduced Wendy. She lost track of the names, too distracted by Porter's warm grasp. Obviously he'd forgotten about their awkward morning after, and she couldn't be more grateful.

"HERE YOU ARE," Porter said when he pulled up to the Come On Inn motel. "This is close to the rodeo grounds, but if you want I'll drive you into town to another motel."

"As long as there are no bedbugs, this should be fine." She opened her door and got out. When he didn't follow, she asked, "Aren't you getting a room here?"

"I'll bunk down in the truck." Since Porter's friend worked on a ranch in the area, he'd insisted Porter use his pickup as long as he needed. Sure beat the heck out of driving the trailer to all his old haunts.

She hesitated, her gaze sweeping across his face before dropping to the gravel lot beneath her feet.

Porter wanted to make love to Wendy again so bad he could still taste her kisses on his lips. Sleeping together once was a mistake—twice would be intentional. They were compatible in bed but nowhere else.

C'mon, Wendy. Close the door.

"This is ridiculous." She glanced sideways as if worried someone was eavesdropping on their conversation. "If you're not going to spend the money on a motel room then you might as well share mine." The look in her eyes promised he'd be sharing more than the room with her.

"I don't think it's a good idea." Someone had to be the strong one. He wanted to be with Wendy again, but he didn't trust his emotions to stay out of the experience. He suspected he was the first cowboy she'd invited into her bed and once the newness wore off she'd leave him in the dust. He knew what it felt like to be used and he wasn't eager for a repeat of that experience.

"Do you do this often?" she asked.

"Do what?"

"Make the girl chase after you?" A pink tinge spread across her cheeks.

He struggled not to smile. "Sometimes." He liked seeing her vulnerable side, which she didn't reveal often. "There's a friend I want to catch up with tonight."

Her eyes widened.

"A guy friend." Hector Flores had been Porter's roping partner for two years on the circuit. Then Hector got his girlfriend pregnant and hung up his rope for full-time work cowboying on the Double Diamond cattle ranch twenty miles south of King City. Porter had texted Hector after he'd arrived at the fairgrounds and asked if he wanted to meet for a beer.

"Wait here." She marched across the lot and entered the motel. Not long after she returned to the pickup and tossed a key card across the seat. "Room 117."

He eyed her cute fanny as she walked off with her overnight bag. Now what? Did he follow her inside, which was what he wanted to do? Or did he drive over to the Salty Dawg Saloon, where he'd promised to meet Hector?

Wendy vs. Hector. That was a no-brainer. He texted

Hector, apologizing for standing him up, then grabbed his duffel and went into the motel. Wendy opened the door almost immediately after his knock. She knew him better than he knew himself.

He moved forward but she blocked his entry. "Are we…?"

"Are we what?"

Her eyes narrowed. "You know…"

Yes, he did know. "There's no other place I'd rather be right now than with you—" he nodded over her shoulder "—in that bed."

She stepped aside and after he passed her, she closed the door and bolted it, as if she feared he'd change his mind. No matter how wrong this was, he'd already crossed the line with Wendy and there was no turning back.

She leaned against the door, eyeing him. Porter wanted to pull her close and tell her everything would be okay and neither of them would get hurt, but he couldn't make that promise.

"I planned to take a shower."

He'd like nothing better than to soap her body beneath the hot spray, but he sensed she needed a moment alone. Since he was a gentleman first and a cowboy second, he said, "Go ahead. I'll wait."

Heart pumping hard, he stared out the window overlooking the parking lot and willed his blood pressure to return to normal. All Wendy had to do was look at him with those dark, sultry eyes, and he was rattled.

Porter pulled a water bottle from his duffel and guzzled half of it. How could one woman—someone he'd known most of his life—turn his world inside out in a couple of days? Doubts crept into his thoughts. There was a part of him that still felt unsure in Wendy's presence, as if he wasn't her equal.

It's all in your head.

Tough to argue with himself when Wendy had given him no reason to believe she felt he was below her. He pictured her cute face, but the image gave way to another woman—a venomous blond bombshell.

Veronica.

As far as his siblings believed, the buckle bunny was history, and she was—except for the fact that he still hadn't forgotten her betrayal. Veronica had used him to make a former boyfriend jealous, knowing all along that he was falling hard for her. What his siblings didn't know was that he'd asked her to marry him. He'd bought a small diamond, but she'd laughed at his proposal.

After the breakup he'd partied hard, hoping the next buckle bunny or the one after her would help him get over Veronica. He'd finally admitted he needed time for his broken heart to heal.

When he was ready to jump into dating again, he picked women who weren't looking for serious relationships, believing that was safer. Then his brothers began traipsing down church aisles with the loves of their lives, and he'd felt left out. He wanted to experience the same happiness his brothers had found, but it wasn't until he'd acknowledged that desire that he'd realized his heart had finally put Veronica to rest. The tricky part now was finding a woman he could trust with his heart.

Darn Wendy Chin and her businesslike prettiness and no-nonsense attitude. If he hadn't slept with her, he'd never have known how good it could be between them.

Give her a chance. She's nothing like Veronica. She's not going to use you.

How could he be sure of that? For all he knew, Wendy viewed him as a good-time cowboy and when they returned to Yuma, she'd leave him in the dust. Veronica had done enough damage to his ego and he refused to let his experience with her taint whatever was happening between him and Wendy. The way he figured, he had a choice—he could tell Wendy he'd changed his mind and didn't want to sleep with her, which would be a lie. Or he could join her in the shower.

He stripped his clothes off and quietly entered the bathroom. The stupid shower curtain was covered in purple and blue butterflies, blocking out Wendy's silhouette. Taking a deep breath, he opened the curtain and stepped inside the tub. "Mind if I join you?"

Her smile enticed him closer. "What took you so long?"

"I have no frickin' idea." He became hypnotized by the stream of water running over her shoulder, between her breasts and down her belly, where it disappeared in the dark curls between her thighs.

"Porter?"

He forced his gaze back to her face. "Huh?"

She inched forward, bumping her body against his. "Would you like me to wash your back?"

He grinned. "I'd rather you wash my front."

She poured shampoo on his head, then lathered his hair before transferring the suds down his body, over his chest around his waist and to his butt.

"That's not my front," he said.

"Patience, cowboy." She moved her hands to his front side, and his head fell back as he groaned. She pressed one finger against his neck. "Your pulse is beating hard."

"That's because your hands are making something else hard."

"Mmm…" She rubbed her nose against his wet throat. The heat from her body set his skin on fire. He fought the urge to sweep her in his arms and carry her into the bedroom and use the bedsheets to dry her off.

"I think it's time to get out," he said. She ignored him and nibbled his earlobe. The feel of her tongue inside his ear sent a bolt of electricity straight to his groin. "Forget drying off." He grasped her waist and spun her until he had her pinned to the wall. "You're driving me crazy." He kissed his way down to her breasts and took his sweet time savoring them while his fingers kept another part of her anatomy entertained.

Her breathing grew labored and not until she clasped his head and forced him to look at her did he realize how carried away they'd gotten. "The water's cold," she gasped.

He turned off the shower, then stepped from the tub and reached for her hand. As soon as her feet hit the bath mat, he swung her into his arms and carried her to the bed. He followed her down onto the mattress but as soon as he stretched out on top of her, she shoved against his chest and rolled him onto his back.

Where the heck had this Wendy Chin—the one who wanted power over him in the bedroom—come from? Her fingers slid up the inside of his thigh, wringing another groan from him. One kiss led to two and then three until they were both breathing hard again.

"Do you know how beautiful you are?" He gazed into her eyes.

"Compliments will get you nowhere."

"What about kisses?"

"Kisses will get you far…very far," she murmured.

He held her against him while he leaned over the edge of the bed and rummaged through his jeans pocket for a condom. Once he sheathed himself, he pulled Wendy on top of him. "Now where were we?"

"We were right here." Wendy's mouth covered his, and Porter let her take him for a ride—a sweet, wild ride.

WENDY LISTENED TO Porter's breathing echoing in her ear. He lay sprawled on his back next to her on the bed, taking up most of the mattress. His arms were spread wide, one hanging off the side, the other pinned beneath her back. He'd thrown his leg over hers during the night, holding her down—not that she cared. She rolled her head sideways and studied his profile.

She braced herself for an onslaught of regrets, but they never materialized. Making love with Porter had been amazing. Maybe it wasn't as unimaginable as she'd first believed to think of being with him long-term.

Great sex doesn't mean a happy marriage.

Marriage? Long-term meant…for a while, not forever. Nothing had changed between when they'd first made love and now—she and Porter were still wrong for each other.

He stretched next to her, and she held her breath. His mouth twitched but his eyes remained closed. She resisted the temptation to brush a lock of hair off his forehead—the need to touch him was unlike anything she'd ever felt for another man. Porter grounded her. Just being in his presence made her more aware of simple things like sunsets and the shape of clouds.

All her life she'd been an overachiever, and her determination and hard work had served her well. But it had also come at a cost. Her job was now her life. How often in the past year had she declined invitations to socialize with her girlfriends? When had she last dropped by Dixie's business and said hello—six months ago? And the only dates she'd gone out on lately were those her father had arranged for her. A lump formed in her throat and a lone tear dribbled onto her cheek. Her job was her life and her life was her job. What fun was that?

Who cares about fun? You're planning for the future.

A future filled with loneliness. She might have a retirement plan and make enough money to live a comfortable life, but she was doing it alone. She willed the negative thoughts away. She was confident she'd eventually find a husband her parents approved of and one she'd look forward to spending her life with. If there was one thing being with Porter had made her realize it was that she needed to reduce her work hours and relax more. How did she expect to find the right man for her if she sat behind a desk all day with her face buried in paperwork?

After tomorrow's rodeo they'd deliver the bulls to their resting place for the next month, then return to Yuma, where she'd inform her boss that Porter had nothing to do with the missing Del Mar bulls.

This trip had ended up being a waste of company money. Her gaze slid to Porter. *Not a total waste.* Just looking at him made her feel happy.

"Why are you smiling?"

She jumped inside her skin. "How do you know I'm smiling? Your eyes are closed."

He blinked then looked at her. "I can feel your smile."

That was the most romantic thing a man had ever said to her. She traced her finger over his naked belly. "I bet I can make *you* smile."

The corners of his mouth quivered. "I bet you can't."

"Is that a challenge?" She scraped her fingernail across his skin, and he sucked in a quick breath, then rolled on top of her.

"Are you sure you're up for that kind of challenge?" He nuzzled her neck.

"Hey, that's not fair." She wiggled beneath him. "I can feel your mouth smiling."

He chuckled. "You can't win this contest unless you see my smile, and there's no chance of that because I'm going to bury my face in all your sweet spots." His mouth teased her breasts, and Wendy's reservations about being with Porter were swept away with his bold caresses.

Chapter Eight

The sweet smell of lilacs drifted past Porter's nose. *Wendy.* He snuggled closer, pushing his body against her softer curves.

A loud buzzing sound echoed through his head, but he refused to open his eyes. He was too comfortable, too warm and too exhausted to wake up. Last night had been incredible. Wendy had shown him her wild side before they'd surrendered to exhaustion and drifted off to sleep in each other's arms.

Hours later she'd woken him with soft caresses and intimate touches, and he'd eagerly given himself over to her again. The third go-round had been accidental. On the way back to the bed after using the bathroom, he'd tripped over his boots and had landed on top of her, knocking the air from her lungs. And she'd made him pay for the blunder—not that he had any complaints about his punishment.

Thinking back on the past twelve hours, Porter admitted that he'd liked making love the third time the best. The sparkle in Wendy's eyes as she'd teased him almost made him forget the reason they'd hooked up was because she was along for the ride, doing her job. For a short while he'd pretended they were the only people left in the world and nothing else mattered but pleasing each other.

The buzzing sound refused to stop, forcing Porter to release last night's memories and open his eyes. He reached for his cell phone on the nightstand, forgetting why he'd set the alarm in the first place. The rodeo didn't end until late afternoon.

"Do we have to get up?" Wendy's muffled voice drifted into his ear.

"I hit the alarm by accident." He tightened his hold on her. "Wanna take another shower together?"

A purring sound escaped Wendy, and Porter tipped her chin up, intent on kissing her. But before his lips touched hers, the song "Good Ride, Cowboy" by Garth Brooks blasted from the phone and he suddenly remembered why he'd set the alarm. "Crap!" He pushed Wendy off him and sprang from the bed.

"What's the matter?" She pulled the sheet over her naked body.

"I'm riding today." He searched for his clothes scattered about the room.

"It's ten-thirty." She groaned and buried her face in the pillow.

"I compete at noon." He took a one-minute shower, then returned to the bedroom. "It's all yours."

Wendy dragged herself from bed and grabbed a change of clothes on the way into the bathroom.

Porter rummaged through his overnight bag and tugged on a clean pair of BVDs and jeans, then sat on the edge of the bed and pulled on his boots. "You almost ready, Wendy?" He hefted his duffel bag over his shoulder and grabbed the keys to his friend's truck.

Wendy stood waiting by the door. She never ceased

to amaze Porter. Any other woman would have been cursing up a storm at not being able to do her hair or put on makeup, but not Wendy. He ran his thumb across the pillow crease marring her cheek, then kissed her. "Thank you."

She blinked. "For what?"

"For a lot of things." He took her by the hand and they left the room.

When they stepped outside the motel, he picked up the pace.

"Race you!" Wendy took off running across the lot, and Porter chased her. When he passed her, she made a grab for his shirt but missed. Laughing, they stowed their bags in the pickup, then Wendy offered him a piece of gum. "Breakfast?"

"Sure." He turned onto the main road leading to the fairgrounds and glanced across the seat. Wendy was a sight—a beautiful mess. Her long hair was still tangled from his fingers running through it all night. Her blouse was untucked. Her lips were swollen from his kisses. And she looked ten years younger without eyeliner.

"I'm sorry." He couldn't believe she wasn't angry at being rudely awakened and hustled out the door.

"For what?"

"I just realized you didn't have to come with me. I could have driven back to the motel and picked you up after my ride."

"Are you kidding? I want to watch you compete." Her smile shot straight through his heart.

When they reached the fairgrounds and parked, he collected his rigging and spurs, then they headed straight for the sign-in table. After he scratched his name on the entry form and learned his chute number, he escorted Wendy to the cowboy ready area. With ten minutes to spare, he sat on a folding chair and put on his spurs. "I'm going head-to-head with Fire and Ice." He nodded to the gelding in the chute.

"She's a beautiful horse," Wendy said.

He stood and put his hands on her hips. "She's a he. How about a good-luck kiss?"

"Porter?" The voice drifting over his shoulder sounded like his sister's.

He froze, his mouth hovering over Wendy's.

"Wendy?"

What were the chances of him and Wendy running into Dixie at a rodeo in California? He stepped away from Wendy. *Damn.* Dixie and her husband, Gavin, stood a few feet away. "What are you two doing here?" he asked.

Dixie noticed where Porter's hand rested—Wendy's waist. Her eyes widened as she took in her friend's disheveled appearance.

"Hi, Dixie." Wendy flashed a shaky smile. "This is a nice surprise."

Dixie frowned. "I can see it's a surprise."

"Hello, Gavin," Wendy said.

Porter's brother-in-law was having trouble containing his grin. Wanting to distract his sister, he asked, "Where's Nate?"

"Staying with Gavin's mother in Phoenix."

"We're visiting one of my army buddies," Gavin said, "and we're competing today for old times' sake."

The announcer called Porter's name and he glanced at Wendy, wishing his sister would disappear so he could claim his good-luck kiss. Wendy offered him a smile instead, and he walked over to his chute, Gavin trailing him.

Dixie pointed to Wendy's chest. "You missed a button."

Wendy glanced down and swallowed a groan, then quickly fixed the problem. Dixie stared pointedly, and Wendy said, "Don't ask."

"You mean don't ask if you slept with my brother?"

"Yes, don't ask that question."

"I thought you were riding along with Porter in a professional capacity, not a personal one."

"I am."

"And part of your job is sleeping with him?" The hostile note in Dixie's voice caught Wendy by surprise. She didn't want to have this conversation, because she didn't know how to answer the question she was positive Dixie would ask—how serious were her feelings for Porter?

"Ladies and gentlemen, turn your attention to chute four. Porter Cash is going to try and tame a rank bronc named Fire and Ice. This horse has made three separate appearances at the National Finals Rodeo in Las Vegas." After the applause died down, the announcer said, "So far in this bucker's career he's managed to toss one hundred and seven cowboys on their backsides before the buzzer."

Forgetting about Dixie for the moment, Wendy moved closer to the chute and watched Porter straddle the horse. Gavin and two other cowboys stood on the rails, ready to help if the bronc grew restless before the gate opened. Fire and Ice stood still while Porter secured his grip, and Wendy wanted to tell him to be careful. Real worry for his safety materialized out of nowhere, making her stomach queasy.

Porter glanced her way, and she offered him a brave smile. He winked, then his chest expanded with a deep breath and he nodded to the gateman. The chute opened and the horse exploded from the pen. Wendy climbed up next to Gavin for a better view.

The bronc twisted then plunged forward and she was amazed that Porter hadn't been thrown. She cringed at the bronc's violent bucking—how could Porter's arm withstand the punishment? In a move that took her and other rodeo fans by surprise, Fire and Ice kicked his hind legs almost past vertical, sending Porter sailing over the bronc's head. He hit the ground hard and rolled.

Wendy's attention remained riveted on Porter, sprawled in the dirt. *Get up!* The bronc continued to buck, making it difficult for the pickup men to release the flank strap. Finally the strap broke free and Fire and Ice trotted out of the arena.

"Looks like that bucker got the best of Porter Cash today," the announcer said. "Better luck at the next rodeo, cowboy."

Porter dragged himself to his feet and stumbled to his hat. He swiped the Stetson off the ground and waved it at the crowd, then hobbled out of the arena. When he returned to the cowboy ready area, Wendy wanted to launch herself into his arms, but she didn't—not with Dixie watching their every move.

"Did you get hurt?" Dixie asked.

"I'm fine." Porter offered a reassuring smile, but Wendy noticed he held his arm close to his side. Crazy man. And for what? He hadn't won any money and he still had to drive the stock trailer later that day.

Now that all the excitement had ended and the fog of their lovemaking had dissipated, Wendy questioned Porter's decision to compete in the rodeo. If his job with Del Mar was so important to him—a way to save money to buy a ranch and raise bucking stock—why would he risk injury and be unable to drive the rig? She was all for having fun and enjoying life, but Porter's decision to enter the rodeo served as another reminder of why they could never go the distance with each other.

"Gavin doesn't compete until later this afternoon," Dixie said. "You two want to grab lunch in town?"

"No, thanks." Porter motioned to a group of cowboys gathering at the next chute. "I'm watching my buddies compete."

Wendy gaped at Porter as he offered her an apologetic shrug—the rat was going to leave her alone with his sister. *Chicken!*

"Fine. C'mon, Wendy. Let's get a hot dog at the concession stand." Dixie narrowed her eyes at her brother. "It is okay if I have lunch with *my friend*, isn't it?"

Porter glared at Dixie. "Wendy can eat with whomever she wants."

Before the siblings got into an argument, Wendy took Dixie by the arm and walked off with her. They cleared the chute area, and then stopped at the first food vendor.

The tension in the air was as thick as the stench near the livestock pens. "You could at least tuck your shirt in," Dixie said.

Wendy obliged without comment. When they reached the front of the line, they both ordered hot dog baskets and diet colas, then sat at a table in the eating area. Wendy was starving—she blamed it on the calories she'd burned in bed with Porter. Hunger aside, she braced herself for an inquisition. In all honesty she wasn't sure why Dixie was so upset at seeing her and Porter together.

"How long have you and my brother been carrying on behind my back?"

"We weren't carrying on behind anyone's back, Dixie."

"Then why didn't either of you tell me you were dating? I thought we were friends."

"We are friends." And because of that Wendy couldn't lie to Dixie. "Porter and I aren't really dating."

Dixie's eyes widened.

"This—" Wendy waved her hand in front of her face "—just sort of happened."

"Nothing *just sort of* happens with you, Wendy."

"What's that supposed to mean?"

"As long as I've known you, you've always had a plan. Your life has been mapped out for you since birth." When Wendy opened her mouth to protest, Dixie cut her off. "I know what kind of life you've had with two demanding parents, so there's no way you'll convince me Porter fits into your future plans or that he's the kind of man your folks would choose for you." Dixie wagged a finger in Wendy's face. "This leads me to the conclusion that you're using my brother."

Wendy gasped, horrified that her friend had such little faith in her. Afraid she'd say something she shouldn't, Wendy counted to five before she spoke. "Porter and I are old enough to make our own decisions about what we do and don't do with each other." Even if those choices weren't smart.

"That's true, but you don't know my brother like I do."

"What are you talking about?"

"I saw the way he looked at you." Dixie played with her drink straw. "He hasn't looked at a woman like that since Veronica Patriot."

The name sounded familiar but Wendy couldn't place it. "Veronica who?"

"Patriot. She was that buckle bunny Porter fell madly in love with a few years ago. She used him to make her ex-boyfriend jealous."

Equal parts rage and heartache filled Wendy. She hated that another woman had been cruel to Porter, but even more she hated that he'd been in love with her.

"After Veronica went back to her boyfriend, Porter never let himself get serious with another girl."

"Then you have nothing to worry about, Dixie. He knows it isn't serious between us." Wendy said the words out loud to convince herself more than Dixie. After only a couple of days together, Porter wouldn't jump to the conclusion that they were in a committed relationship. Or would he?

"Are you sure he understands? I don't want to see him get hurt again."

"I hear what you're saying, Dixie, and I applaud your loyalty to your brother, but this isn't any of your business."

Her business or not, Dixie wouldn't drop the subject. "I don't get it. He's not even your type. Porter didn't go to college and he can't hold down a job for very long."

Angry that Dixie had so little faith in her brother, Wendy said, "You don't know him as well as you think."

"What do you mean?"

"Did he tell you that he's saving money to buy a ranch so he can start raising roughstock for rodeos?"

Dixie laughed. "Porter lives in a fantasy world.

Grandma Ada left all of us kids a share of her life insurance after she died, and Porter was the first one to blow through his five thousand dollars. He talks a good game, but he'll never save enough money to buy a ranch. Not unless he wins the lottery." Dixie grasped Wendy's hand. "Please don't hurt him. Even though he doesn't have his act together, he's a good guy."

Porter was a good guy—Wendy was discovering just how good with each day, hour, minute and second they spent together.

"If you need a reminder that he's not the right man for you, then introduce him to your parents. That should settle the matter."

As much as Wendy wished to reject the idea, Dixie was right. Her parents would never accept Porter, and even if she overcame their objections to him, she couldn't say for sure that he was the right man for her. He was fun, entertaining and he could make her laugh, but was there such a thing as having too much fun? Would she grow weary of being the responsible one in their relationship? Of being the one who worked long hours to make enough money to support them because Porter floated from job to job?

Maybe he'll change for you.

But then he wouldn't be the same man who'd swept her off her feet.

Feeling a headache coming on, Wendy rubbed her temples. Was it only a couple of hours ago that she'd woken in Porter's arms, relaxed and satiated? "I get what you're saying, Dixie."

"It's not just Porter I'm worried about."

Wendy eyed her friend warily.

"We've known each other since junior high. You're

smart, savvy and climbing the career ladder. You were born to do well and you deserve your success. You've worked hard to get where you are and you need a man who'll believe in you and support your efforts."

Was she saying Porter wouldn't approve of her career goals?

"You need a man who's as determined as you to succeed, and Porter is not that guy."

Good grief. If all the Cash siblings believed Porter was a screwup and would never accomplish anything in life, no wonder he'd never reached for his dreams before now. "Don't underestimate your brother."

"I'm not." Dixie traced a scratch on the tabletop with her fingernail. "Porter's a fun guy—the kind everyone wants at their party. But few people know he has a sensitive side and he feels things deeply."

"What do you mean?"

"Just that he has a big heart. Despite all your differences, he could still fall in love with you. Then when you decide to move on, he'll be devastated."

Porter would be horrified if he heard his sister talking about him like this. "I'll take what you've said under advisement."

Dixie changed the subject. "How many of these trips do you have to make with your clients each year?"

Not wanting to give Dixie more ammunition to fire at her, Wendy lied. "Not many."

"What happens when you return to Yuma?"

"I write up a report, then my boss takes it from there."

"Is Porter doing okay? I mean, he hasn't done anything wrong, has he?"

"I'm not critiquing Porter," Wendy said. "I'm documenting how Del Mar Rodeo moves its roughstock from one event to the next. Rodeo bulls are a big business and there's a lot of money invested in them."

"No kidding. Shannon's been after Johnny and her father to breed rodeo bulls." Dixie smiled. "I don't think Johnny realized what a handful Shannon would be when he married her."

"You'd think little Addy would keep Shannon too busy to think about rodeo bulls," Wendy said.

"Don't tell anyone, but Shannon's pregnant."

"Really?"

Dixie pressed a finger to her lips. "Mum's the word. I'm the only one who knows…well, you, too, now."

"Why is she keeping it a secret?"

"Because Marsha just found out she's pregnant and Shannon doesn't want to spoil the excitement for Will and Marsha after they make the announcement to the rest of the family."

"How many years will there be between their son, Ryan, and the new baby when it's born?"

"Seventeen."

"It'll be like raising an only child again." The talk about babies and pregnancies sent a wistful stab of longing through Wendy. As much as she loved working, she wanted to be a mother one day. But the possibility seemed far off with no potential husband in the picture. "What about you? When do you and Gavin plan to have another child?"

"Nate with all his ear infections is enough for me to handle right now. As soon as we get him healthy again, we'll work on a second baby."

"You ladies gonna sit here and jabber all day or do you want to watch the bull-riding event?" Gavin stopped next to Dixie's chair and placed his hand on her shoulder. Porter hung back a few feet, his gaze skipping over Wendy.

"Did I miss your ride?" Dixie asked Gavin.

"Yes, ma'am, you did."

"I'm sorry." Dixie hugged her husband. "How did you do?"

"Not so good." Gavin kissed Dixie's cheek, and the couple walked off, leaving Porter and Wendy alone.

"Are you okay?" Porter asked.

"Sure. Why wouldn't I be?"

"Dixie tends to stick her nose where it doesn't belong."

"We're fine. Let's watch the bull-riding competition." Better to be with Porter in a crowd than somewhere with too much privacy. After discussing him with his sister, Wendy wanted to hug him close and ask for a kiss.

"Sure."

As they walked to the stands, Wendy noticed that Porter was still cradling his arm close to his side. "Is it your shoulder or elbow?"

"Shoulder."

She appreciated that he didn't try to joke about his injury. "You hit the ground hard when you fell off the horse."

"I didn't fall off. I got bucked off."

"Same difference."

"Not really," he grumbled.

She snagged his shirtsleeve, and he stopped. "Maybe you should go to the first-aid tent and have one of the paramedics look at it."

"I said it was fine."

"I know, but—"

"If you're concerned I won't be able to drive the truck, don't worry. I'll manage."

Miffed, Wendy released his shirt and followed him to the stands. How could he believe she was more concerned about his driving than his health after what they'd shared at the motel?

Porter ushered her into the bleacher seats next to Dixie and Gavin. After the first bull ride, he murmured in Wendy's ear. "I'm sorry. I'm in a grumpy mood."

"It's okay. I wouldn't be happy if I hurt myself, either."

"It's not that. It's Dixie's bad timing."

Amen to that.

"She thinks she knows what's best for everyone," he said. "I hope she didn't butt her nose into our business."

This was not a conversation to have with the subject sitting close by. Wendy pointed across the arena to the livestock chutes. "Which one is a Del Mar bull?"

"Riptide. He's coming out of chute three. He's the one that was left inside the barn at Bell Farms."

When the bull exploded from its prison, Wendy paid more attention to the animal than the crazy cowboy on its back. "What's so special about Riptide?"

"No cowboy has ever ridden him to the buzzer." And right on cue the bull tossed his rider. Luckily the cowboy managed to scramble to his feet and dodge the bull's attempt to trample him.

"Looks like Riptide's gonna keep his perfect record intact," the announcer said. "Mark my words, folks. You'll see this bull at the National Finals Rodeo in December."

Riptide was good—better than good—and would

bring in top dollar in breeding fees. Was that why Big Sam had hidden the animal in the barn at Bell Farms?

"Happy Hour is coming out next," Porter said. "He's not one of Del Mar's."

Wendy sat straighter. Happy Hour was the name of the bull Glen Fenderblast said Buddy was interested in purchasing.

"Is Happy Hour for sale?"

"A bull is always for sale, if the price is right. Hank thinks Buddy will make an offer as soon as he gets enough money together."

"What's Happy Hour got that Riptide doesn't?"

"Longevity. Riptide has two, maybe three years left on the circuit. Happy Hour's young and because he's off to a great start in his career, the talk is that he'll be worth a couple million by retirement."

Wendy's mind raced back to just before Christmas of last year, when Buddy had requested a quote for increasing the insurance coverage on his bulls. Had he been setting his plan into action before he'd even filed a claim for the first missing bull?

The pieces of the puzzle were slowly coming together, and things weren't looking good for Buddy. But Wendy found it difficult to believe he might be involved in a scheme to defraud his insurance company. He had a solid reputation in the ranching community. Ask anyone—and she had made several inquiries—and no one had a negative thing to say about the man. It was possible her boss was grasping at straws.

Kind of like you and Porter.

Wendy was not grasping at straws with Porter.

She didn't need to find reasons to be hopeful that things would work out between them—she knew they wouldn't. So why was it so tough for her to accept that?

Chapter Nine

Late Sunday afternoon Porter watched Wendy out of the corner of his eye as the rodeo helpers loaded the Del Mar bulls into the stock trailer. She'd been quiet since Dixie and Gavin had departed two hours ago. Talk about rotten luck—his sister showing up out of the blue after he and Wendy had spent the night together. He was certain Dixie had commented on Wendy's disheveled state, but he was too chicken to ask what his sister had said.

"Here you go, Cash." The rodeo helper handed him the livestock paperwork. "Loaded and ready to go."

"Thanks." It wasn't until the man walked off that Porter realized he hadn't checked the bulls' numbers as they entered the trailer. *Damn it.* Wendy Chin had a way of messing with his head even if she didn't speak a word. He walked over to the trailer and unlatched the door.

"What are you doing?" she asked.

No sense fabricating a lie—she'd see through him. "I was too busy thinking about you…us…last night…I didn't pay close attention to their numbers."

Wendy's gaze softened. "I did. They're all Del Mar bulls."

"Thanks." It was nice to know she had his back, but obviously he hadn't made an impression on her or she'd have been just as preoccupied by their lovemaking last night as he'd been. "I shouldn't have zoned out." He hadn't touched her in hours and couldn't resist tucking a loose strand of hair behind her ear. He trailed his finger down her neck. "You're amazing."

She batted her eyelashes. "Amazing how?"

"Nothing rattles you." He grinned. "You'd make a great business partner." He envisioned having Wendy at his side, helping him run his roughstock business. And at night after she shut down her computer and the broncs had been fed and watered, they'd sit on the porch and watch the sunset.

"Speaking of business, why are you delivering the bulls to Baker's Landing and not taking them back to Buddy's ranch?"

"The veterinarian at Baker's Landing will check the animals over and make sure they didn't suffer any injuries at the rodeo, then they'll be turned out to pasture for a month to rest."

"Why don't they rest at Buddy's?"

"Hank has this group of bulls scheduled to compete in four weeks at a rodeo two hours north of Baker's Landing. The less traveling the animals do, the better they perform, so it makes sense to keep them in California until then." He motioned to the truck cab. "Need a hand up?"

"No way. I'm a pro at this now." She opened the passenger door, stepped back and leaped forward, bracing one foot on the front tire as she propelled herself into the air. She caught the handhold and slid onto the passenger seat. "Told you."

Porter closed the door and hopped in behind the wheel. As soon as he cranked the engine, Wendy opened her iPad. She worked the entire drive to Baker's Landing and continued after they left the ranch, stopping only when Porter pulled up to a taco stand south of King City. "I'm hungry."

"Me, too." She closed the tablet and got out of the truck, then lifted her arms above her head and stretched.

Porter made no apologies for ogling the way her shirt pulled tight against her breasts. Sitting in the truck with her had been torture. Focusing on traffic had been exhausting when he couldn't stop thinking about Wendy in his bed.

After ordering food they sat at a picnic table beneath the shade of a tree. They were five hours from Yuma—he wished they were ten. He didn't want the trip to end. On a whim he said, "How would you like to see the ranch I want to buy? It's on the way home."

"I'd love to see it."

He'd never taken any of his brothers or Dixie to the property, because he knew they'd shoot down his dream and call him crazy. Porter wasn't sure how Wendy would react, but regardless he wanted her to know that he was thinking about his future.

The drive to the Fortuna Foothills area east of Yuma was uneventful except for the jackknifed trailer that caused them a half-hour delay. As he navigated the winding trails, they passed four ranch entrances before the road leading to Morning Sunshine Ranch came into view. "Here we are."

He turned onto the property and drove beneath the sign with the ranch's name carved out of metal.

"Pretty name for a ranch. Would you change it?" she asked.

"I don't know."

"Who owns the property?"

"The bank."

"You'd think they'd want to get the land off their books and would be willing to sell it dirt cheap," Wendy said.

"The price is reasonable, but the property needs a lot of updates."

Porter slowed down, and Wendy studied the land with a critical eye. Other than an abundance of mesquite trees, which would provide shade for livestock, and clusters of prickly pear cactus, the terrain was far from inviting. Porter parked in front of a faded red barn. The horse weather vane on the roof was missing one of its legs. Rusted pieces of ranching equipment littered the yard and an old Ford pickup with flat front tires baked in the sun.

"It's close to the entrance to the property," she said.

"Makes for a short drive in and out for the stock trailers." Porter took Wendy's hand, and they walked behind the barn, where a double-wide trailer sat.

She eyed the contraption propped up on cinder blocks. "What's that?"

"The ranch house."

Porter had to be kidding. The Arizona sun had faded the once maroon-colored mobile home to pink and dents the size of bowling balls peppered the side. She followed him up the wooden steps to the door.

"Be careful," he said when the platform wobbled beneath their feet.

The first thing Wendy observed when she entered

the trailer was the bare windows, which allowed the sun to stream into the room.

"It must be over one hundred degrees in here," she said.

"A fresh coat of paint would make it look nicer."

Paint—how about a wrecking ball?

He waved her into the kitchen. "The appliances have to be replaced, but the cabinets are in good shape."

Was he seriously considering living in the trailer if he purchased the property?

"I know it's not your stereotypical ranch house, but it comes with the property. Once I got my roughstock business off the ground, I'd build a new home."

Wendy considered her apartment, which she rented from her parents and how they monitored her every move. There was something to be said about having your own home, no matter if it was a two-story house or a rusted-out trailer.

The door squeaked open, and she and Porter spun.

"Hey, George." Porter stepped forward and shook the older man's hand.

"See you brought someone to look at the place with you. And ain't she as pretty as a summer daisy."

Wendy held out her hand. "Wendy Chin."

"Pleased to meet you, ma'am." He removed his hat. "I'm George Jones."

Wendy's eyes widened.

"Porter 'n' me got a lot in common. My full name's George Jones McAndrews. George Jones wasn't yet singin' when I was born, so you can't accuse my mama of naming me after the legend. George was my daddy's name and Jones was my granddaddy's name."

"George watches over the property for the bank," Porter said.

"We were just admiring how spacious your home is," Wendy said.

"This ain't mine. I bunk down in the barn."

Wendy sent Porter a puzzled look, and he explained, "George used to work for the previous property owners."

"The McCalls went bankrupt in '98 and moved back to Iowa," George said.

Ninety-eight? The man had lived on the property for over a decade?

"You still got your eye on buyin' this place?" George asked.

"I'm hoping to approach the bank with an offer this fall."

"You let me know. I can whip this ranch back into shape."

Wendy doubted the old cowboy could whip anything with his hunched back, bowed legs and arthritic hands.

"I'll hold you to that promise, George. I'm going to need a good hand to help with the livestock."

"I rode a few broncs in my younger days." George winked at Wendy. "Just a handful of years ago."

Wendy laughed at the geezer's flirting.

"You two enjoy your visit here."

The door hadn't even closed behind George before Wendy said, "How does he manage out here in this heat?"

"I brought him an old generator last year. He hooks it up to an industrial fan when it becomes too warm to sleep at night."

"You've been checking up on him for a year?"

Porter nodded. "When I toured the property and discovered he lived in the barn, I brought out a few pieces of furniture that Grandma Ada had left in the attic." He shrugged. "George is like family."

Wendy could understand how he'd bonded with George. Porter's grandfather Ely Cash had passed away years ago and Dixie had mentioned once that Porter didn't know the identity of his birth father.

"Don't worry about George. There's a well on the property, and the water's safe to drink. He manages okay."

"He must get lonely." Wendy pictured the old man sitting on a cot in the barn, waiting day after day for Porter to drop by.

"He still drives. If he gets lonely, he heads into town and bothers the waitresses at the Waffle House."

"But the tires on his truck are flat," she said.

"The pickup doesn't belong to him. He drives a 2001 Toyota Camry."

"And he doesn't have any relatives who look after him?" Wendy found it difficult to believe the man didn't have anyone in his life—except Porter.

"George never married or had kids."

"How old he is?"

"Seventy-six. Give or take a couple of years."

"It's obvious he cares about you," she said.

Porter rubbed the side of his nose and stared at his boots. "Knowing that George is waiting for me to buy the place helps keep me focused on my goals." He removed his wallet from his jeans pocket and set two twenty-dollar bills on the kitchen counter.

"You have everyone fooled, Porter."

"What's that supposed to mean?"

"Your siblings all believe you're a goof-off and irresponsible, but you're taking care of an old man who's not even related to you." He held open the trailer door and she stepped outside. "You're a softie at heart."

"That doesn't sound like a compliment," he said.

Wendy grabbed the front of Porter's shirt and pulled him toward her until their mouths touched. She used her lips to tell him everything her heart wanted to say. When they broke apart she said, "You're the nicest man I've ever met."

And whoever lands you for a husband is going to be a very lucky woman.

THE FOLLOWING DAY Porter entered his sister's business in downtown Yuma. "Dixie?"

No customers browsed Dixie's Desert Delights, but clanking sounds echoed from the kitchen at the back of the gift store. He weaved through the display stands of perfumed soaps and lotions, then hovered in the doorway. Dixie stood in front of the sink, pouring one of her soap concoctions into molds.

Now that she and Gavin had moved away from the farm and purchased a house in town, he didn't see her as often. "We need to talk."

Dixie barely glanced up from her task. "Go away, Porter. This is hot and I don't want to burn myself."

He held his tongue and his temper until she finished her task then set the pan aside and gave him her full attention. "What's wrong?"

"Where's Nate?" He didn't want to wake his nephew if the kid was napping.

"He's having a playdate with a preschool friend."

Good. Porter could get right to the point. Even

though he was older than Dixie, she treated him as if he was the baby of the family and needed coddling. "What did you say to Wendy at the rodeo last weekend?"

"What are you talking about?" She turned her back to him and wiped off the countertop.

Wendy had become unusually quiet after he'd given her a tour of Morning Sunshine Ranch. She hadn't said more than a sentence or two on the way to the pecan farm to pick up her car. He'd expected a goodbye kiss, but she'd barely managed to look him in the eye when she got into her car and drove off, which didn't make sense after she'd kissed him at the ranch.

"Wendy's not returning my calls." Porter had been ignored by a few ladies he'd pursued over the years, but Wendy's cold shoulder stung. If she didn't want to see him again, wouldn't she tell him? "Wendy and I were getting along fine until we ran into you and Gavin at the rodeo."

Dixie planted her hands on her hips. "When are you going to grow up, Porter?"

Whoa. Where had that come from?

"Wendy is way out of your league. I don't even know what she was thinking when—"

"She had sex with me?"

Dixie blushed.

"Maybe she was thinking she was attracted to me. Or that she liked me. Or that she wanted to be with me." Was that such a stretch?

Dixie snorted. "Obviously she was attracted to you or she wouldn't have slept with you."

"And you assume that sex is all there is between us."

"You're my brother and I love you, but sometimes you don't have a clue."

He shoved a hand through his hair. "Forget about the sex. Wendy and I had a lot of fun together."

"She'd have had fun with any guy that wasn't Asian."

"What's that supposed to mean?"

"How much has she told you about her upbringing?"

"I know she has a college degree and she's smart." *And making a hell of a lot more money than me.*

"Wendy's parents expect her to marry a Chinese man."

"She told me. It's a cultural thing. And her parents are putting pressure on her to marry sooner rather than later."

Dixie stared hard at Porter, and a sick feeling gripped his stomach. "Are you saying…?" Shoot, he couldn't even finish the sentence.

"I don't know if Wendy was with you for the thrill of it or a final fling before she resigns herself to settling down with a man her parents pick for her." Dixie rubbed her brow. "I guessed that you two had slept together and my protective instincts kicked in and I warned her not to hurt you."

"You *warned* her away from me?"

She nodded.

Porter appreciated his sister's concern, but he was a grown man. "I can handle myself, Dix. I don't need you to fight my battles." Did the rest of his siblings believe him incapable of looking out for himself?

"I remember how badly Veronica hurt you."

"I'm over Veronica. I have been for a while." Porter drew in a deep breath, praying for patience. "Wendy is nothing like Veronica." He forced the words past his lips, wanting to believe them, but Dixie had already planted a seed of doubt in his mind. "You're forgetting that Wendy's an adult. She can choose whatever man she wants to be with."

"Fine. Maybe Wendy defies her parents to be with you. But even if her folks get past the ethnicity issue—" Dixie abruptly closed her mouth.

"Don't stop now," he said.

"Porter, you're a fun-loving, laid-back guy. Of course Wendy would find you intriguing."

"Intriguing?"

"You're unlike any man she's ever dated."

"Go on."

"You're easygoing—the opposite of Wendy, who's a go-getter."

"I'm not disputing that Wendy's good at her job. So what?"

"It's more than that. She's an overachiever and you're an underachiever. There's no way you two would ever be happy in the long run. You'd both frustrate each other."

That's how his family viewed him—as an underachiever? "I've changed, Dixie. You've seen how I help Mack at the dude ranch, and I lend Johnny a hand during spring branding. And now I'm hauling rodeo bulls."

"But for how long? Until something more interesting comes along? Then you're off chasing after another job or not working at all." Dixie crossed the room and hugged Porter. "Don't worry. You'll find the right woman one of these days."

In the past he would have gone along with whatever his sister said, because he preferred to take the path of least resistance. But after getting to know Wendy and making love to her, he was in a fighting mood. And Wendy was worth fighting for. He didn't know if they had a future together, but he sure as heck believed they needed to allow their relationship to run its course and not let anyone but them decide if they should or shouldn't be together.

"As much as I appreciate your concern, little sister, butt out of my personal life." He spun on his boot heels, but her voice stopped him.

"Porter. Whatever you do…don't hurt Wendy and please don't ruin my friendship with her."

To Porter's way of thinking, he was the one more likely to get hurt. He left the shop, hopped into his truck, then sat and stared out the windshield.

The only way to learn if Wendy was distancing herself from him because of Dixie's warning or because she'd decided they were through was to talk to her. And since she refused to accept his calls, he had to find another way to communicate with her.

A woman pushing a baby stroller passed the truck and when Porter saw the bouquet of flowers shoved in the basket beneath the seat, an idea came to mind.

He drove through town and parked in front of the Lotus Flower Shop on Main Street. A giant pink lotus had been painted on the front window, along with the store hours and a phone number. A planter overflowing with red and white blooms sat next to the door of the brick building.

Tapping his finger against the steering wheel, he went over in his mind what he'd say to Wendy's mother or father, but everything he rehearsed sounded stupid. He'd just have to wing it.

When he entered the store, sleigh bells attached to the handle jingled. An Asian woman appeared behind the counter and smiled. For an instant he believed he was seeing Wendy thirty years from now.

"Good afternoon," she said. "Welcome to the Lotus Flower. How may I help you?"

He approached the counter. "I'd like to send a bouquet to a special lady."

The older woman's eyes sparkled. "Tell me about the lady who's captured your heart."

He smiled. "She's beautiful and has long, dark silky hair."

"What is her favorite color?"

The question stumped Porter. "I'm not sure. Maybe go with a mixed bouquet."

"I'll use gerberas, yellow daisies and purple asters."

Porter knew what a daisy looked like. He wasn't sure about the other two flowers. "Throw in a few red roses, too."

Mrs. Chin frowned. "Roses are expensive. Are your feelings for her serious?"

"Yes, ma'am."

"How much would you like to spend?"

"How much should I spend to impress a lady?"

Wendy's mother studied him as if determining the amount of money he carried in his pockets. "Thirty dollars."

Irked that she assumed he was almost broke, he pulled his wallet out and placed a hundred dollars on the counter.

Smiling, she said, "Would you like to wait while I make the arrangement?" He nodded and she disappeared into the back room. Porter strolled through the shop studying the various arrangements until his feet grew tired, then he sat on the bench in front of the window and watched traffic drive by on Main Street. Twenty minutes had passed when Wendy's mother returned with a humongous bouquet. Porter was a cowboy, not a flower connoisseur, but he recognized a striking arrangement when he saw one.

"You're very talented," he said.

"Would you like to send a note with the flowers?"

He supposed that was the appropriate thing to do, but he was no poet and figured he'd only make a fool of himself if he attempted anything romantic.

To a new beginning. That sounded stupid.

Thanks for the fun. She'd think all he'd cared about was the sex.

"How about 'Looking forward to spending more time with you,'" he said.

Mrs. Chin wrote out the note. "How would you like me to sign the card?"

He opened his mouth to say his name, then caught himself. "Just sign it from the cowboy."

"The cowboy?"

Obviously she thought he was nuts. "She'll know who I am."

"Where would you like the flowers sent to?"

"American Livestock Insurance Company."

Wendy's mother glanced up. "A name?"

"Wendy Chin." After dropping the proverbial bomb, he tipped his hat. "Have a good day, ma'am, and thank you for your help." He glanced at the store as he backed out of the parking spot and caught Mrs. Chin watching him through the window, her brow creased with worry.

Boy, would he like to be a fly on the wall in Wendy's office when the flowers arrived.

Chapter Ten

"You believe the driver has nothing to do with the missing bulls?" Carl Evans asked Wendy. Her boss had called her into his office late Wednesday afternoon when he'd returned from a business trip to Phoenix. This was the first chance they'd had to discuss the Del Mar case since she'd gone on the ride-along.

"Porter Cash is innocent of any wrongdoing." Wendy had emailed Carl a copy of her report following the trip to Colorado and California—but she'd omitted the stop at Morning Sunshine Ranch. She was still trying to reconcile the Porter she knew from high school with the one who'd given money to a lonely old cowboy. The one who was no longer living life by the seat of his pants but had big dreams for the future.

"I'm disappointed," Carl said.

"Why?"

"I wanted the culprit to be a greedy livestock hauler taking payments on the side. Now we have to investigate this Big Sam you said acted suspicious."

"Have you shared my report with the sheriff?" Wendy had included a note detailing how she suspected Big Sam of trying to switch out a Del Mar bull with one from Bell Farms.

"I sent a copy to the sheriff's office, but I don't expect any action soon. His secretary said he's knee-deep in a drug-smuggling case."

When Wendy had taken over the Del Mar account, she'd learned that cattle rustling was more widespread than commonly believed, but unless a person was killed in the act of stealing livestock, the investigation process proceeded at a turtle's pace. Missing cows were low on the list of priorities for law enforcement in a town located close to the Mexican border.

"If I don't uncover concrete evidence that Buddy Davidson is trying to swindle us, I'm going to have to cut a check to Del Mar Rodeo," Carl said.

"Porter mentioned that Buddy plans to buy a bull named Happy Hour. I saw the animal compete in King City."

"Buddy's always in the market for new bulls."

"Maybe, but this one is special. Happy Hour's value could be well over a million dollars."

Carl straightened in his chair. "That's why Buddy asked you to increase his insurance coverage."

"We can't accuse him of filing fraudulent missing-livestock claims until he collects enough money to finance a million-dollar bull," Wendy said.

"We need to speak with Buddy. He's bound to—" Carl narrowed his eyes. "How well did you get to know Porter Cash on this trip?"

The blood drained from Wendy's face, then a second later flooded back into her cheeks. Had someone told Carl that she and Porter had shared a motel room? "What do you mean?"

"Cash may be our best bet for finding out what Buddy's up to."

"How?"

"Ask Cash to chat with Buddy. Maybe his boss will let something slip."

Wendy didn't like the idea at all. She didn't want to put Porter in the middle of an insurance investigation. Besides, if Buddy became suspicious, he might fire his driver, and Wendy didn't want to be responsible for Porter losing his only source of income—and possibly jeopardizing his ability to buy the ranch in the Fortuna Foothills.

"Get in touch with Porter," Carl said. "Set up a date. Buy him a few beers, then ask if he'll help us."

"I don't feel comfortable doing that." Aside from being unethical, if she hung out with Porter, she'd end up in his bed again. And Dixie would be even more furious if she discovered Wendy had asked Porter to spy on his boss to help with the insurance investigation.

"Take him to dinner at the new steak house out on the highway." He snapped his fingers. "What's it called?"

"The Golden Steer."

"Butter him up with a few drinks and a fillet and he'll cooperate."

"There's got to be another way to get the information out of Buddy," she said.

"Wendy."

"What?"

"You're having dinner with Porter Cash this Friday. Make it happen." He shoved a stack of papers into his briefcase. "Jared has a soccer game tonight. I better get going."

"Wish him luck." Wendy returned to her desk, where she stared unseeingly at the computer screen. What excuse could she use to contact Porter after she hadn't returned any of his calls since they'd gotten back to town?

Drat. She was torn over her feelings for the cowboy. After their road trip, she'd been caught off guard by how much she'd missed his company. And she missed the simple things, like the way he tapped his finger against the steering wheel when a song he liked came on the radio. The way he stretched his arm across the back of the seats and toyed with a strand of her hair. The way he put his hand against her lower back when they entered a store. Most of all she missed his smile. Porter smiled at everyone—friends, strangers, waitresses and convenience store clerks. But when he smiled at her, there was an intimate glimmer in his brown eyes that warmed her blood and made her feel special. All he had to do was grab her hand and say "C'mon" and she was ready to follow him to their next adventure.

And when they'd made love…Porter was the first man she'd been willing to give up control with in bed. The sex with Tyler hadn't been half as exciting as her experience with Porter, and she'd loved Tyler. Wendy's blood pumped faster as she dreamed of a happy-ever-after with Porter—not that it would ever happen.

"Got a surprise for you."

Wendy glanced up and came face-to-face with an explosion of color. Sherry, the company receptionist, placed the flower vase on Wendy's desk. "They're gorgeous. I didn't know you were dating anyone."

"I'm not."

"Well, I'm jealous. I've never received an arrangement as beautiful as this one." Sherry nodded to the card. "Aren't you going to open it and see who sent them?"

Not in front of the office gossip. Wendy pushed the vase to the back of her desk. "I need to make a call first." She reached for her cell phone, and Sherry left, closing the door behind her.

Wendy's gaze zeroed in on the telltale lotus flower etched into the crystal vase. *Oh, my God.* What had gone through her mother's mind when Porter walked into the flower shop and ordered the arrangement?

With trembling fingers, she opened the card and read her mother's handwriting. *Looking forward to spending more time with you. The Cowboy.*

She didn't know whether to laugh or cry. Porter hadn't given away his name—unless he'd paid for the flowers with a credit card. She pressed a fingertip to her smiling mouth, picturing her mother's reaction when he told her where to send the flowers. Her heart warmed with admiration for Porter. He hadn't allowed the fact that her parents wanted her to marry a Chinese man intimidate him.

She stroked a velvety rose petal, thinking the arrangement must have cost a fortune. She hated that Porter had spent his hard-earned cash on something that would end up in the trash in a week—except for one stem. Wendy would keep a souvenir from the arrangement—a single rose pressed between the pages of her favorite book, *The Secret Garden.*

Porter really cares for you.

Porter was unlike any of the men her father had chosen for her. Those men had been business savvy, and thought nothing of using people to reach their lofty goals. Porter didn't use others to get ahead. He helped people, even if it meant sacrificing or delaying his own goals.

She pressed her nose to the flowers and breathed in their sweet scent. There was much to admire about Porter. Not only his kindness toward others—she'd also caught a glimpse of an iron will beneath his live-for-the-moment attitude. There was no doubt in her mind that one day he'd own the Morning Sunshine Ranch. A part of her wished she could be at his side when he achieved his dream.

She'd call Porter and thank him for the arrangement, then ask him out to dinner because she wanted to see him again—not because her boss had told her to. She took a steadying breath and dialed his number.

"Hello, darlin'."

His sexy voice rattled her. "Porter, um…"

"You get the flowers?"

"They're beautiful."

"Not as beautiful as you."

She smiled. "You shouldn't have spent the money."

"If you're worried I can't afford them, let me—"

"No, no. That's not it." Darn it, she was messing up badly.

"Are you concerned about your parents?" he asked.

"Maybe a little." *More like a lot.*

"I hope I impressed your mother."

"Oh, I'm sure you made an impression." *Probably not a good one.*

"You two look alike."

"So we've been told."

"How come you haven't returned my calls?"

"I've been busy writing reports since we got back to town."

"All work and no play, huh?"

"Not necessarily," she said. "I'd like to take you to dinner this Friday."

"You don't have to buy me dinner to thank me for the flowers."

"That's not the reason."

"Oh?"

"I wanted to thank you for putting up with me on the trip."

"I didn't have a choice."

He wasn't making this easy. "And because I enjoyed being with you." That was the truth. She ignored the prick of guilt at not telling him the invite was also work related. "I thought we could try the steak house that opened—"

"The Golden Steer."

"That's the one."

"When?" he asked.

"Let's meet there at seven."

"I'll pick you up. Dixie told me where you live."

How would her parents react when Porter showed up on her doorstep? "See you then." She disconnected the call and stared at the flowers.

Her phone beeped—a text from her mother.

Who is this cowboy?

She'd love to ignore her mother, but if she didn't explain the situation between her and Porter, her parents would show up at her office demanding answers.

I'm on my way to the flower shop.

Wendy shut down her computer and left the office. As she drove across town, she tried to think of a valid reason for Porter to send her flowers, but she doubted her parents would believe anything she said. She parked behind the flower shop, then entered through the back door. Her mother and father were waiting for her.

"Who's the cowboy?" They spoke in unison.

They didn't allow her to answer. "He's not Chinese," her mother said.

"No, he's not. And the arrangement was beautiful, Mom. You did an amazing job."

"Don't think you're going to distract us, young lady." Her father peered over the rim of his bifocals.

"Porter Cash."

"Dixie's brother?" her mother asked.

"Yes."

Her father frowned. "The Cash brothers' reputations leave a lot to be desired."

"You can't believe half of what you hear," she said. "Except for Porter, the brothers are all married with families."

Her mother glared. "*The cowboy* isn't—"

"Porter and I are just friends." *Friends with benefits.* "He's a livestock hauler for Del Mar Rodeo, which you know is my client. I did the ride-along with him last week."

"Why would he spend a hundred dollars on flowers if you're just friends?" her mother asked.

"He was appreciative of me trying to figure out why Del Mar's bulls are disappearing."

"I don't care about missing bulls." Her mother stamped her foot. "And a simple thank-you would have been enough." She pointed her finger at Wendy. "He wants more than friendship from you. No man spends that kind of money on flowers if he doesn't have feelings for the woman."

Wendy wasn't going to come out ahead in this conversation.

"And what did he mean by looking forward to spending more time with you?" her father asked.

"I have to do another interview with Porter."

Her parents exchanged frowns, then her father asked, "Where is this interview taking place?"

"The Golden Steer. Friday night."

"Sounds like a date," he said.

"It's a business meeting, and Carl suggested it."

"Carl's not your father. I am and this is a bad idea."

"I understand your concerns, but I can look after myself."

"You shouldn't be seen alone with Porter," her mother said. "You have to watch your reputation."

"None of the men Dad has set me up with has heard of the Cash brothers. And what you don't know about Porter is that he's a really great guy. He's not the playboy you think he is."

Her father narrowed his eyes. "Is this your way of rebelling against me?"

"What are you talking about?"

"I introduced you to two respectable men this past year and you found something wrong with both of them."

How could she admit she was struggling with accepting a man her father chose for her? He'd be disappointed in her attitude, assuming she didn't believe he knew what was best for her, which in turn made Wendy feel terrible after all her parents had sacrificed to give her a good life.

*Your parents love you. They'll learn to accept who-
ever you choose to be with.*

Deep down Wendy believed that, but she ignored the
voice in her head and told herself that pleasing her parents was her first priority—a safer choice. After having her heart ripped to shreds by Tyler, she didn't trust
her judgment or her heart not to fail her again. It was
better to marry a man her parents approved of than to
take a chance on loving Porter.

"Maybe we should move." Her father ignored her
mother's gasp. "If we sell the business and relocate to
California, you'll have more men to choose from."

"You can't sell the flower shop," Wendy said. "You
love Yuma. This is home." She rubbed her brow, feeling
the familiar headache come on, as it always did when
the three of them got into an argument about her future.

"Stop worrying," she said. "When I find the right
man you'll be the first to know."

"The right man better not be Porter Cash." Her mother's words followed Wendy out the door to her car and
all the way home.

"You must be going somewhere special if you're pol-
ishing your boots," Conway said after he entered the
bunkhouse late Friday afternoon.

"I'm meeting Wendy Chin for dinner." Porter caught
the way his brother's face tightened. "What's the matter? The babies keeping you and Isi up all night?"

"The girls are sleeping in five-hour stretches now."

"That's pretty good." Porter set aside one boot then
picked up the other. "So why the funny face?" When
Conway didn't answer, he said, "Dixie talked to you,
didn't she?"

"How did you know?"

Porter buffed his Ariat, taking his frustration out on the boot.

"She's worried you're getting in over your head with Wendy."

"You'd think our sister had enough on her plate with being a mother and wife and running her own business that she wouldn't have the energy to stick her nose into my life."

"You know Dixie. She worries about everyone in the family."

"I suppose your wife has an opinion about my love life, too," Porter said.

"Are sleeping with Wendy?"

Obviously Dixie had left out that part when she'd spoken to their brother. "What if I am? It's no one's business what Wendy and I do together."

"You're right. Back to your original question…Isi thinks it's great that you're dating Wendy."

Porter wouldn't call it *dating*. Actually, he had no idea what to label their relationship. After the road trip ended and he didn't hear from Wendy, he'd worried that he didn't mean as much to her as she meant to him. That's why he'd sent the flowers. He'd wanted her to know she hadn't been a fling. He'd also hoped the bouquet would convince her to pick up the phone and call him. And his strategy had worked.

Now if only he could get over the attack of nerves that had hit him this morning when he'd crawled out of bed. A sixth sense insisted Wendy planned to call it quits between them before their relationship got off the ground and he wanted to convince her to give what they'd shared the past week a chance to grow. He tugged on his boots and stood. Conway looked as if he had more to say. "What else is on your mind?"

"The strangest thing happened the other day. I helped Johnny haul horses to a ranch north of Scottsdale and on the way home we stopped for a beer at the Horseshoe."

"What's strange about that?"

"We ran into Hank Martin at the bar."

"Yeah, so?"

Conway's gaze shifted to the rodeo posters decorating the wall. "Johnny should probably talk to you about this."

"For crap's sake, Conway, spit it out." Porter had less than an hour before he was supposed to pick up Wendy.

"Johnny thinks that maybe Hank Martin is your father."

A jolt of icy heat shot through Porter's chest. He thought back to the afternoon in the bar when Hank had taken the stool next to him and struck up a conversation. If Hank was his father, why the heck had he waited almost twenty-eight years to reach out to Porter? "What makes Johnny believe Hank is my dad?"

"He asked a lot of questions about you."

"What kind of questions?"

"Like if you'd ever tried to find your father."

How could Porter have looked for the man when he didn't know his name? "What did you tell him?"

"That you hadn't searched for the man." Conway's brow scrunched. "You haven't, have you?"

"No."

"Johnny wants to look into Martin's background."

"Leave it alone. You guys will end up getting me fired."

"What are you going to do?"

"Why do I have to do anything?" Porter shot back.

Conway backed toward the door. "Hey, don't shoot the messenger."

Porter regretted losing his temper. "Tell Johnny not to worry about me or Hank Martin."

"Sure." Conway hesitated. "If you need us, we're always here for you."

After his brother left, Porter sat on the bed and stared into space. No way was Hank Martin his father. They didn't look alike—then again, Porter took after his mother's side of the family. His gut insisted he wasn't related to Hank—but why all the questions? The next time he spoke with Hank, he'd ask if he was his father.

Then again, maybe he should leave well enough alone. He wasn't sure anymore if he wanted to know the identity of his biological father. How would his siblings feel if he was the only brother who had contact with a parent? Maybe it was best to leave well enough alone and not ask Hank why he was poking his nose into the Cash family tree.

It had only been him and his siblings all these years. They'd struggled through good and bad times together. They didn't always get along, but in a crisis they closed ranks, and Porter didn't want that to change. As the youngest he'd always complained that his brothers had gotten in his grill too much, but he'd liked the attention and he'd understood the harassment had been their way of showing they cared. If he formed a relationship with his biological father, Porter worried his siblings would stop lecturing and giving advice. In truth he'd rather have Johnny, Mack, Conway, Buck, Will and even Dixie tell him what to do any day than take the word of a stranger who'd wanted nothing to do with him all these years.

He checked his watch, then splashed cologne on his neck before grabbing his hat and keys. The drive to Wendy's lasted forty-five minutes. He parked on the street and took a few moments to study the duplex. A handrail separated the porches of Wendy's apartment and her neighbor's. There would be no privacy for a good-night kiss later.

He strolled up the sidewalk and rang the bell. A movement out of the corner of his eye caught his attention and the curtain shifted in the window of the neighboring apartment.

Wendy opened the door, and Porter nearly swallowed his tongue. "Red looks great on you." He grasped her hands, then kissed her cheek. She smelled good, too. "You grew a few inches since I last saw you."

She lifted her foot, and he admired the black stiletto pumps. "Sexy." He hoped she'd invite him inside— mostly because he wanted to start the date off with a bone-melting kiss, but she disappointed him when she stepped onto the porch and shut the door.

He reached for her hand to help her down the steps when the neighbor's door opened and a familiar-looking woman poked her head outside.

"Mom, I believe you and Porter have met. Porter, this is my mother, Li Chin."

Caught off guard, Porter removed his hat. "Hello, Mrs. Chin. Nice to see you again."

The older woman's eyes flashed with silent messages Porter couldn't interpret.

"This is my father, Jun Chin," Wendy said when a man joined her mother on the stoop.

Porter offered his hand. "Nice to meet you, sir."

Wendy's father nodded but didn't speak.

An awkward silence followed, and finally Wendy spoke. "I'll see you both later." She slid her arm through Porter's, and they walked to his pickup. He opened the door for her and helped her inside then waved at Wendy's parents as he rounded the hood and got behind the wheel.

He started the engine. "I don't think they approve of me."

"They don't."

He glanced at the duplex as he pulled away from the curb—Wendy's parents stood like stone-faced statues.

"I guess it's a good thing you approve of me," he said.

The silence that followed his statement was deafening.

Chapter Eleven

The hostess at the Golden Steer seated Porter and Wendy in a corner booth, then took their drink orders and left them to peruse the menu.

Porter reached across the table and clasped Wendy's hand, threading his fingers through hers.

The feel of his callused hands sent a surge of yearning through Wendy and it took more strength than she imagined to *not* suggest they skip dinner and spend the evening at the bunkhouse on the farm. She wished he hadn't brought up the flowers. As beautiful as they were, the arrangement made her feel guilty for allowing things to go too far between them, especially when she'd known from the beginning that a relationship with Porter would be problematic for her parents.

"You're not mad that I sent the flowers, are you?"

"No." She wasn't upset with Porter, she was angry at her parents and herself. She reminded herself that this was a business dinner, but everything having to do with Porter had become personal. "The bouquet is beautiful but it rattled my mother and father." And Wendy, too.

"My intent wasn't to aggravate your folks," he said.

She drew in a steadying breath. "My parents are old-school." Old *Chinese* school. Even though they were both born in the States, their parents were not."

"What does that have to do with us being together?"

"Both sets of grandparents had trouble assimilating into American society and moved from place to place looking for work."

"Why did your mom and dad settle in Yuma?"

"My mother's parents were making their way to California when they stopped in Yuma and noticed a Help-Wanted sign in the window of the flower shop. They were almost broke so my grandmother applied for the job and the owner hired her. When the delivery boy quit, my grandfather took over that job. Years later the owner, Mr. McHenry, passed away and my grandparents purchased the shop."

"What happened to your father's parents?"

"They settled in California and my grandfather worked on the docks in San Francisco. He died in a dock accident when my father was in his early twenties. After his death my grandmother returned to her family in China and my father remained in America."

"I guess your father left California, too."

"He was visiting a friend in Yuma when he saw my mother outside the flower shop. He said it was love at first sight."

"Don't tell me he became a flower delivery boy."

She laughed. "No. He convinced my grandfather to hire him to work with his suppliers. My father had to prove to my grandfather that he was worthy of my mother. It took him three years to win my grandparents' approval."

Porter's expression sobered. "Once your mom and dad get to know me, they'll change their minds about us being together."

Wendy couldn't help but admire Porter's cowboy cockiness. If only hard work and guts were all it took to rope her parents in.

"You're smiling. That must mean I have a chance." Like a bucket of cold water dumped on her head, his words shocked her back to reality.

"Uh-oh. What happened to the smile?" When she didn't answer, he asked, "Are you afraid I'll say or do something to offend them?" He released her hand and sat back in his chair. "I'll be on my best behavior."

She wanted to cry. Everything inside her insisted that Porter could be *the one* for her, but she didn't have the courage to defy her parents. If she continued seeing Porter, she'd be forced to pick between him and her parents. And honor would win out.

Honor? That's bull and you know it.

Startled by the voice in her head Wendy dropped her gaze and held her breath, sensing her conscience had more to say.

Quit blaming your parents. You're the one who believes you can't be with Porter. You're the one afraid to take a chance on him.

"We should take your folks to a rodeo."

Wendy shushed the voice in her head and gave her attention to Porter. "They've been to a couple of rodeos, but it's not really their thing."

"What are their hobbies?"

"Work." Porter didn't understand that her parents' whole world revolved around the flower shop. The waitress saved her from having to explain. After placing their orders, she said, "It's not a good idea for you to hang out with my parents, Porter."

His smile dimmed. "Why not?"

Wendy's heart ached for him. For them. For what they'd never have.

This felt like a breakup date, but how could that be when they weren't really a couple? Finding the words to convey how much she cared for him but that nothing could come of those feelings was next to impossible.

"Let's just say my parents aren't much fun. They don't know how to have a good time."

"I can pour on the charm when I need to."

She knew firsthand how lethal Porter's charm could be. If she didn't change the subject, she'd end up in tears. "I need your help."

His smiled disappeared. "What's going on?"

"Earlier today Buddy filed an insurance claim with us for another missing bull."

"Which one?"

"One we delivered to the King City rodeo."

"No frickin' way."

"It's the bull Big Sam hid in the barn at Bell Farms," she said.

"Riptide." He shook his head. "All the bulls were accounted for when we dropped them off at Baker's Landing. You can vouch for me."

"I assured my boss that you had nothing to do with the missing bull."

"Who do you suspect took the animal?"

"I don't know. We turned over the information to the sheriff's office, but our case isn't a priority right now."

The waitress arrived with their meals. Porter waited until she filled their water glasses before he spoke. "You said *another* missing bull. How many have disappeared?"

"A total of four."

His stare burned into her. "I knew it."

"Knew what?" she asked.

"Your ride-along with me was more involved than you led me to believe."

"Yes."

He stabbed the knife into his steak and cut off a chunk. She didn't blame him for being miffed at her. "I couldn't tell you the whole truth because you might have accidentally said something to the wrong person, who would then have tipped Buddy off that we were investigating him for insurance fraud."

"Buddy doesn't know he's a suspect?" Porter asked.

"He doesn't know his insurance agent is investigating him. The sheriff's department already questioned him."

The muscle along Porter's jaw pulsed angrily. "Did you believe I was involved?"

"No!" At his doubtful look, she confessed, "In the beginning I didn't know if you were involved or not, but I'd hoped you weren't."

"Why?"

"Because you're the brother of a good friend and…"

"And what?"

She jutted her chin. "Because I like you."

"How do you know I didn't help the bad guys steal the bulls?" He set aside his fork. "I'm saving money to buy a ranch. Maybe I'm getting a kickback from my boss for playing dumb." He pointed his finger. "I can tell by the look on your face that you were thinking that."

"Are you involved in anything illegal?"

Anger sparked in his eyes. "Hell, no."

"I didn't think you were." She held his gaze, willing him to believe her.

"What convinced you that I had nothing to do with the missing livestock?"

"It wasn't any one thing. It was more of a feeling."

"What kind of a feeling?" When she didn't answer, he asked, "Did this feeling come before or after we made love?"

Wendy's face flamed. "Before." Her answer knocked some of the steam out of his mad, and his stiff posture relaxed.

"Why do you believe Buddy's involved?" he asked.

"I'm not a hundred percent certain he is involved, but both you and his neighbor mentioned that he has his eye on buying Happy Hour—"

"Whoa." Porter held up his hand. "You can't convict Buddy on something he said in casual conversation."

Why was Porter defending his boss? "I realize that, but when you add four insurance claims together, Buddy would have enough money to purchase or finance a prized bull."

"I wish you would have been up front with me from the beginning. I might have paid closer attention to what was going on around us during the road trip."

He was taking this a lot better than she'd expected.

"What's your next move?" he asked.

"My boss was hoping you'd agree to visit Buddy's ranch and see if you can get him to talk about the missing bulls."

"So that's what this dinner is about…asking me to spy on Buddy?" Porter's stare bored into her.

Wendy let him believe that because it was easier, but Porter was only partially right. She and Carl did need his help, but even if they hadn't, Wendy would have found an excuse to see Porter one more time before she walked away for good.

"I've been working for Del Mar Rodeo less than three months," he said. "Buddy's not going to confide in me."

"What about Hank Martin?" Porter looked surprised by her question.

"Do you suspect Hank of foul play?"

"We can't rule out any of Buddy's employees. Besides, Martin hired you."

"What does that have to do with you suspecting Hank?"

"He hired and fired two of Del Mar's livestock drivers in the past nine months. After each driver had been let go, Buddy filed an insurance claim for a missing bull."

"And now you're wondering if Hank will fire me after a bull disappeared on my watch?"

"There's nothing to suggest he wouldn't if we don't find that bull."

"I'm heading out on the road next Thursday," he said.

"Where to?"

"Deming, New Mexico."

"Could you speak with Hank before then?" she asked. "Maybe you can get him to tell you why he fired the other drivers."

Porter didn't respond to her suggestion. Instead, he said, "Have you contacted the fired drivers and interviewed them?"

"As soon as Buddy called about the second missing bull, my boss hired a private investigator to look into Buddy's employees. When the drivers were questioned, they claimed they'd lost their jobs because of complaints about their driving." The investigator believed the men were lying, but there had been nothing suspicious about their actions after they'd left Del Mar Rodeo, so he'd crossed the men off his list of suspects.

Porter picked up his fork and knife and cut into his steak. Wendy let him eat in peace while she picked at the food on her plate. The steak was tough and the potato too soggy. She left half her meal untouched. When the waitress checked back with them and asked if they'd like to order dessert, Porter declined.

Wendy handed the waitress her company credit card and after she signed the receipt, they left the restaurant. The drive to her apartment took forever. After Porter parked on the street in front of the duplex, he stared out the windshield.

Wendy hesitated, then reached for the door handle, but he grabbed her arm, stopping her. "Did being with me mean anything to you, or was I nothing more than a job perk?" he asked.

Sitting in front of her parents' home wasn't the proper place for this conversation, but she gathered her thoughts, realizing that no matter how she phrased her words, they'd still hurt him. "What we shared meant something to me, Porter."

"I sense a *but* coming."

"But you and me…it just won't work."

"You're going to have to come up with a different reason we can't be together than your parents believing you can do better than me." He glanced at her. "You're twenty-six years old, Wendy. You're free to choose who you want to be with."

"It's not that easy."

"None of this makes sense." He shoved a hand through his hair. "Sometimes I wonder if you're using your parents as a scapegoat because you can't be truthful with me."

Darn him. Porter was *not* going to make her confess that she was falling in love with him. She couldn't give him that kind of power over her, because she knew if he set his mind to convincing her that they belonged together he'd win. "You don't understand our culture."

"Then help me understand." He brushed his fingers across her cheek and swept a strand of hair behind her ear. "Because I don't want to walk away from what we started." He leaned across the seat and kissed her mouth—a gentle brush of the lips. "When I'm with you, I don't feel like anything's missing from my life."

He was going to make her cry. "It's more complicated than convincing my parents to accept you."

"There's nothing complicated if two people care for each other and want to be together."

It hadn't passed Wendy's notice that both she and Porter had avoided confessing their love—neither one of them wanted to be the first to say *I love you*. She recalled Dixie's story of Veronica Patriot breaking Porter's heart and understood his fear and reluctance to be caught in that position again. She'd had her heart broken in the past, too, and she didn't wish that pain on anyone.

"Is there someone else?" Porter asked.

"No."

"But there was," he said.

"My senior year of college."

"What happened?"

She might as well tell him. "His name was Tyler. He was from Tucson."

"Was he Asian?"

"No."

"Did your parents approve of him?"

"They didn't know about him." She swallowed the painful lump that formed in her throat. It still hurt to talk about Tyler's betrayal. "We began dating at the beginning of our senior year and before Christmas he told me that he loved me. By spring break he was dropping hints that he intended to propose."

"Did he?"

"Yes. But not to me."

Porter's eyes widened. "Seriously?"

"Tyler had proposed to a girlfriend back home. I was a college fling until he graduated."

"I'm sorry he hurt you." Porter's mouth brushed across Wendy's again, and it took all her strength to resist deepening the kiss. "I don't understand what your old boyfriend has to do with why we can't be together."

"I realized that even if Tyler hadn't been two-timing me, we would have broken up eventually because my parents would never have accepted him." That was the reasoning Wendy had used to help the wounds heal faster.

"You can't give your parents that kind of power over you, Wendy. You should decide what man you want to be with."

"I love and respect my parents. You wouldn't understand."

"I wouldn't understand because I don't know who my father is or because my mother was a tramp?"

"No!" She expelled a frustrated breath.

He drummed his fingers against the steering wheel. "This is it then. We're not seeing each other anymore?"

Wendy fought back tears. "It's best if we remain friends."

He laughed, the bitter sound hitting her like a punch in the face.

"If you knew all along that you would never allow things between us to become serious, why'd you sleep with me?"

"A girl can dream, can't she?" Wendy got out of the truck and hurried up the sidewalk to the door. The sooner she entered her house, the sooner she could cry her eyes out.

AT ONE O'CLOCK on a Saturday afternoon, the Horseshoe Saloon was dead. Only two customers had walked through the door since Porter sat down at the bar—a past-her-prime female dressed from head to toe in spandex and a rumpled salesman who'd joined the woman at her table.

Porter had stopped by the bar on the off chance that he'd run into Hank Martin. He admitted he was curious as to why Hank had questioned his brothers about Porter's birth father, but mostly he hoped to glean information that would help Wendy's case. Even though she'd ended their relationship, he still cared about her—a lot. And he cared about keeping his job. If he got saddled with the blame for the missing bull, he could kiss his dream of owning Morning Sunshine Ranch goodbye.

Porter stared at the half-empty bottles of booze lined up behind the bar and tried to make sense of his dinner date with Wendy last night. He was equal parts pissed off and embarrassed. Embarrassed that it hadn't been a real date—at least in Wendy's mind—and pissed off that she'd refused to stand up to her parents and fight for him. Them.

You had fun but she's done with you.

Porter winced.

Dixie warned you.

His sister had reaffirmed what Wendy had already told him—her father would choose who he wanted his daughter to be with. And Porter hadn't a clue how to convince Mr. Chin to give him a chance to prove he was worthy of Wendy.

He'd sent the flowers to show Wendy's parents that his intentions toward her were serious, but instead of gaining their favor, he'd alienated himself. He didn't know how to fix the mess he'd made but he wasn't ready to walk away from Wendy. Deep down he believed she cared about him and had only ended their relationship to please her parents—not herself.

"Mind if I sit down?" Hank Martin stood next to Porter's stool.

Well...well...well. It looked as if he'd have a chance to question Hank after all. "Sure."

Hank caught the bartender's attention and pointed to Porter's beer. The barkeep delivered the drink then returned to watching the Diamondbacks baseball game on the TV.

"Got any big plans this weekend?" Hank asked.

"Nope. How 'bout yourself?"

"Nothing exciting."

Not wanting this opportunity to slip through his hands, Porter asked, "How long have you worked for Buddy?"

"'Bout seven years."

"What did you do before that?"

"Ranch work where I could find it."

"In Yuma?"

"California."

"Were you born there?"

"Mississippi." Hank picked at the label on the bottle.

Before Porter poked his nose into Hank's job at Del Mar he had a few personal questions he wanted answered. "My brothers said you were asking about our family and my mother."

"I'm not who you think I am," Hank said.

"Who would that be?"

Hank stared Porter square in the eye. "Your father."

Before he'd processed the information, Hank landed another blow. "But there's a good chance Buddy Davidson is."

Porter had thought about how he'd react if he ever discovered the identity of his birth father, but the strange numbness spreading through his chest wasn't what he'd imagined. "What makes you believe that?"

"I was with Buddy when he met your mama across town at the Cadillac Café."

Johnny and Mack had discussed their mother's various attempts at holding down a job—employment that never lasted more than a few weeks before she left town with the next love of her life.

"Your mama…" Hank smiled. "She was a looker. And she knew just how to make Buddy believe he was the one."

Porter didn't know what to say to that. He knew his mother had made a lot of men think they were special.

"Buddy took Aimee out on a proper date and introduced himself to your granddaddy."

"How do you know all this?"

"We doubled-dated. That night I was with a gal named Samantha. We stopped at the Cash farm to pick up your mama. Your granddaddy didn't seem too interested in anything Buddy had to say." Hank guzzled his beer then belched. "It was common knowledge that your mama loved men, and Buddy wasn't her first rodeo. I suppose your granddaddy knew even before Buddy did that Aimee wasn't going to keep him long."

"What happened?"

"Aimee and Buddy dated for a month. When Aimee turned up pregnant, Buddy offered to marry her."

Had Buddy loved Aimee Cash or had he proposed to her out of a sense of duty? "Let me guess," Porter said. "My mother turned him down."

"Yep."

"Did she say why?"

By now Hank had peeled the label clean off the beer bottle. "Aimee told Buddy she couldn't marry him because she was certain her true love was waiting for her just down the road or around the next bend or across the river. Take your pick."

That sounded like something Porter's mother would say. "What happened after she rejected Buddy?"

"He asked what your mama planned to do about the baby, and she insisted she'd take care of it. Buddy figured that was her way of saying she'd get an abortion."

Why would Buddy have thought that when Porter's mother had kept all the other children she'd gotten pregnant with? *Maybe he was looking for a way out.*

"Not long after that, Buddy and I got into an argument." Hank shrugged. "Can't remember what it was, but I took off back to California. Didn't make my way here again until after your mama passed on."

Porter would have been almost twelve.

"Buddy and I let bygones be bygones, and he gave me a job working for Del Mar Rodeo." Hank drained his beer. "By then Buddy had convinced himself that your mama had had the abortion and that you were the offspring of that someone more exciting around the next bend."

"What makes you think I'm not?"

"Have you checked your reflection in the mirror? You have your mama's hair color but your nose and jaw are Buddy's."

Porter hadn't paid any attention to Buddy's looks when he'd interviewed for the job. "Did Buddy ask you to encourage me to apply for a job at Del Mar Rodeo?"

Hank nodded. "I think the guilt finally got to him. He wants to get to know you better."

"What if I'm not his son?"

"I don't think that matters anymore. Buddy accepted that you were his son years ago."

Porter couldn't figure out why Buddy had waited all this time to reach out to him. "Why are you telling me this and not Buddy?"

"Because he doesn't want to pressure you into finding out if the two of you are related."

Porter wasn't sure how he felt about the possibility of being Buddy's son. Still dealing with the fallout between him and Wendy, Porter shoved aside the news and switched his focus back to the missing-bull investigation. "Do you have any idea why Buddy has trouble keeping drivers on?"

Hank stiffened. "What are you talking about? He pays his haulers more than most stock contractors."

"I heard about the drivers who got fired after making only one run," Porter said.

"Speeding tickets." Hank slid off the stool. "You're scheduled to run a load of bulls to New Mexico next."

"I know." Hank must have forgotten he'd emailed him the trip details last night.

"Leave the girl behind this time."

The beer bottle froze halfway to Porter's mouth. "How did you find out about my passenger?"

"Big Sam mentioned her when we spoke on the phone."

"Is there a rule that says I can't have a *girlfriend* ride along?"

"Liability issue."

"Why didn't someone tell me that when I was hired?"

"I'm telling you now." Hank pulled six dollars from his pocket and tossed them onto the bar, then headed for the exit. He stopped when he reached the doors. "I was sorry to hear about your mama's passing." Then he was gone.

Holy cow. Wait until he told his brothers that it wasn't Hank Martin who'd fathered him but maybe Buddy Davidson.

Chapter Twelve

Wendy's cell phone went off at one in the morning, waking her. "Hello?"

"You busy?"

Porter. Automatically her lips spread into a smile. "I was sleeping."

"You want me to call back in the morning?"

"I'm awake now. What's wrong?"

"I ran into Hank Martin tonight."

"Where are you?"

"Parked behind your parents' flower shop."

"I'll meet you there in twenty minutes." After disconnecting the call, Wendy brushed her teeth, splashed her face with cold water, then tugged on a pair of black-and-pink Victoria's Secret sweatpants and matching T-shirt. Then she put on her eyeglasses and sneaked out of the duplex.

There was no way to disguise the noise of the car engine as she drove past her parents' bedroom window. So be it. It wasn't as if she was making a booty call in the middle of the night. This was an emergency business meeting—part of her job. In truth, she hadn't been able to forget the hurt look on Porter's face when she'd told him she couldn't continue to see him, and she would have jumped at the chance to meet him no matter what hour of the morning it was.

When he'd dropped her off after dinner Friday night, her parents had bombarded her with questions. She hadn't appreciated the interrogation, so she'd banned them from her apartment and gone to bed early, only to toss and turn until she finally fell into an exhausted sleep. Tonight had been a repeat of the same— lecturing parents and no sleep.

When she turned out of the driveway, the porch light flickered on—her mother and father would be waiting up for her when she returned. She really ought to consider moving across town.

When she pulled into the lot behind the flower shop, Porter was sitting on the tailgate of his truck. Their gazes connected as she stepped from the car. He didn't smile—not that she expected him to greet her with enthusiasm. "I found out who my father might be tonight," he said.

Startled, Wendy was momentarily speechless.

Porter straightened his shoulders and clenched his jaw. Wendy wasn't buying the tough-guy stance—not when his eyes flashed with uncertainty. He needed a hug and she needed to hug him. She inched closer and when he pulled her against him, she breathed a sigh of relief. Nothing in the world seemed impossible and everything felt right when Porter held her. They hugged for a long while, and then she asked, "Is it Hank?"

"No." He dropped his arms and she felt a chill rush over her. "Buddy Davidson," he said.

Wendy hadn't seen that one coming.

"I can tell you're as shocked as I am." He shoved a hand through his hair.

"I've known Buddy for almost three years and never would have guessed he had a son." She shook her head. "Even the investigator my boss hired to look into his background never came across any information about him having a child."

"Hank said Buddy dated my mother for a month before she ended up pregnant. She told Buddy she'd get an abortion after he offered to marry her." Porter slid off the tailgate and paced in front of her car.

"I don't understand why Hank told you this and not Buddy," she said.

"Me, neither. Hank claims Buddy's worried about my reaction."

"Maybe you should speak to Buddy before you get too invested in the idea." Wendy didn't want to see Porter get hurt. "You won't know for sure you're father and son unless Buddy takes a paternity test."

Porter stopped pacing. "You're right. Maybe Hank made it up."

Wendy doubted the supervisor would toss out paternity information unless he was confident his claim was true, but it wasn't her place to say. "Did Hank tell you anything about the drivers that were fired?"

"He acted surprised I asked about the men, then paid for his beer and walked out of the bar. I don't think he cared for my questions."

"Would you like to grab a coffee somewhere and talk about Buddy?"

"Not really." Porter cupped her face in his hands, lifting her head until they stared into each other's eyes. "I like you in glasses. You should wear them more often." Then he kissed her—nothing heavy or romantic. Just a gentle meeting of the lips, leaving her yearning for more. "What I want to talk about is us."

The urge to flee was sudden and swift, but there was nowhere to run. She'd spent the past twenty-four hours alternating between crying and cursing at the unfairness of life. Her defenses were weak, and she didn't trust herself to stick with her decision to end things with Porter. The desire to ignore her parents' wishes was as strong as ever—maybe stronger after all she'd been through with Porter.

He rested his forehead against hers. "If I ask you a question, will you give me an honest answer?"

"Yes."

"Do you care about me?"

"Yes." *More than you'll ever know. More than I can let you know.*

"Prove it. Give me a chance to convince your folks that my intentions toward you and them are honorable."

They'd already had this conversation, but she gave Porter credit for being persistent—not only with his words but his lips. He settled his mouth over hers and this time he kissed her slow and deep. His arms cradled her in a protective embrace—as if he could keep the bad in the world at bay. When he let her come up for air, she gasped for breath.

"It won't work," she said. "My parents are set in their ways." *And Porter still hasn't told you that he loves you.*

"I'll change their minds."

If only it was that simple.

He brushed a strand of hair from her eyes. "Are you worried I'll say or do something to offend them?" He kissed her forehead. "I'll be on my best behavior."

He was going to make her start crying again. The need to be with Porter was powerful, but the fear of having her heart broken again was stronger, and she took the coward's way out, blaming her parents. "You won't change their minds about you."

A dark mask slid over his face, and he released her. She'd hurt him again, but better now than to give him false hope. "You said you were driving to New Mexico next Thursday. I'd like to go with you." This trip would be on her dime and she'd have to use a few vacation days, but she wanted badly to prove Buddy wasn't breaking the law. If he was, Porter would lose his job and the means to buy his dream. Not to mention that if Buddy was Porter's biological father, Porter would be crushed if he was involved in something illegal. And the sooner she solved the mystery of the missing bulls, the sooner she'd be able to put Porter behind her and move on to wherever she was meant to be.

"You can't come with me," he said.

"Why not?"

"Hank knew you were along on the last trip and warned me not to bring any *girlfriends* with me again."

Great. What else did Hank know that they didn't? "I'll follow in my car."

Porter opened his truck door. "Do what you want."

"When are you leaving?"

"I'm picking the bulls up at seven a.m. at Buddy's ranch."

"I'll wait for you out on the highway."

Porter revved the pickup's motor, then sped off, leaving Wendy close to tears again. She had a feeling she'd be doing a lot more crying as soon as she solved this case.

"I'M GLAD YOU guys could make it tonight." Porter spoke to his brothers gathered at the table in the bunkhouse. He'd invited them over for a poker game Sunday evening, wanting to share what he'd learned about Buddy.

"Times like this," Johnny said, "I wish Buck and Destiny lived closer."

Buck was the only brother absent and Dixie hadn't been able to make it out to the farm because little Nate had had tubes put in his ears yesterday. The tubes were supposed to decrease the number of ear infections—the poor kid was always sick and running a fever.

Mack shuffled the cards. "I'll deal first."

Conway's phone beeped with a text message and he grinned.

"What is it?" Will asked.

Conway held up the phone, showing a picture of his twin daughters, Emma and Mia, lying in their cribs, fast asleep.

"I can't believe how you've taken to fatherhood," Johnny said.

His brothers teased Conway until Porter cleared his throat. "Since we're talking about fathers—" He waited until he had everyone's attention. "I might have found out who mine is."

"I thought you didn't care if you knew the identity of your father," Johnny said.

"I don't care." Porter picked up his cards.

Mack laid his hand facedown on the table. "Then how did you find out who the man is if you weren't searching for him?"

"Someone told me."

Conway and Johnny exchanged knowing glances.

"It's not who you think," Porter told them.

Will scowled. "Who do they think it is?"

"Hank Martin."

"Why would it be Martin?" Mack asked.

"Johnny and I ran into Martin at the Horseshoe bar and he asked a lot of questions about Porter and Mom," Conway said.

"If it's not Martin then who is it?" Johnny asked.

"Buddy Davidson."

"I don't get it," Will said. "Why would Martin tell you this and not Buddy?"

"I bet Buddy was too chickenshit to tell you himself," Mack said.

"Buddy asked Martin to tell me because he didn't want to put any pressure on me if I wasn't interested in reaching out to him."

"Talk about awkward," Will said. "You work for the man."

"What are you going to do?" Johnny asked.

"You've got to confront him," Conway said. "Ask him why the hell he waited twenty-eight years to come forward."

"He doesn't have to confront anyone if he doesn't want to," Will said.

Porter understood where Will was coming from after his brother had faced down his own father and been cruelly rejected. Sure, Porter was a lot older than Will had been when he'd stood up to his birth father, but that didn't mean he was any less worried or nervous.

If he didn't know who his father was, he didn't have to risk being rejected—at least not in person. Now that Porter knew there was a good chance he was Buddy's son, he had to deal with the possibility that Buddy wouldn't live up to his expectations. "I haven't decided what I'm going to do."

"Shoot," Mack said. "Davidson's been living right under your nose all these years."

"Just say the word, Porter. We'll help in any way you need us to," Johnny said.

"I appreciate that."

Conway picked up his cards. "Whose turn is it?"

"I'll go." Will tossed a card away and tapped his finger for a new one. The conversation centered on his brothers' kids and their wives and whether or not they should have a barbecue at the farm on Labor Day.

Porter recalled a few years ago when the conversation at the table had focused on buckle bunnies, bars and Mack's music gigs. Life sure had changed for the Cash brothers, and Porter was feeling left out. He wanted what his siblings had—a wife, kids and the love and security of his own family. And he wanted it all with Wendy.

After two hours of card playing, Johnny tossed his hand down and stood. "I'm beat."

"What's the matter?" Porter said. "You used to stay up until three in the morning then catch a catnap and rise at five to feed the cattle."

"You wait, Porter," Johnny said. "When you marry and have kids, you add a whole lot of worrying to your daily chores. You'll be ready for bed at ten o'clock every night."

"Sounds like trouble at home," Mack said.

Johnny shook his head. "Not trouble. Shannon's just been cranky lately and I don't know why, because Addy's behaving like an angel."

"Yeah, well, if you figure out why your wife's

cranky," Will said, "let me know because Marsha's been grumpy, too. I work all day fixing other people's houses and then I have to come home and tackle a list of so-called little projects she keeps coming up with."

Conway chuckled. "You guys are the older brothers, but you're both stupid."

"Shut up, Conway," Johnny said.

"Do I need to spell it out to you?" Conway asked.

"Spell what out?" Porter asked.

"Shannon and Marsha are probably pregnant." Conway grinned. "When Isi was pregnant she was a like a hornet flying around me, just waiting for me to screw up so she could poke that little stinger in me."

Will's face lost all color as he sat in a trancelike state. Johnny was grinning from ear to ear. "Will, you okay?" Porter asked.

"I don't know." Will sucked in a deep breath. "I never thought Marsha and I would have another kid together."

Mack slapped him on the back. "This time you'll be around to help raise your son or daughter."

"Hey, maybe you guys should ask your wives if they're expecting before you rush off to buy baby booties and pacifiers," Porter said.

"Guess I'll head home and find out," Johnny said.

The brothers filed outside to their pickups. Conway waved goodbye as he went inside the farmhouse, then shut off the porch light. One by one the downstairs rooms went dark, and the only light remaining was in the upstairs bedroom window.

Johnny drove off first since his truck blocked the others. Then Mack followed. Will scuffed his boot against the ground and leaned on the hood of his truck.

"What's the matter?" Porter asked. "Did all that talk about babies scare you?"

"A little."

"Don't worry, Will. You'll be a good dad. Look how you and Ryan are getting along now. It's like you raised him from day one."

"But I didn't. Marsha did."

"And she'll help you through it. Trust her. I doubt she'd have allowed herself to get pregnant if she didn't have faith that you'd be a great dad to another baby."

"Speaking of fatherhood...you were awfully quiet after you broke the news about Buddy."

"Wouldn't you be caught off guard if your father had been living right in your backyard all these years?"

"I suppose, but I thought maybe your pouty face had something to do with a woman." The corner of Will's mouth curved upward.

"Damn Dixie. She told you about me and Wendy?"

"No, she told Marsha when she had lunch with her, Isi and Beth." Just like the brothers got together for poker when they could, the wives planned lunch dates and gossiped about husbands and kids.

"Sheesh. Everyone in the county will know that Wendy and I had a fling."

"Fling? Marsha made it sound a lot more serious."

Porter had never opened up to Will. He'd always gone to Johnny for help and advice, but maybe Will was the best brother to talk to, because he'd experienced a similar issue with his wife, Marsha.

"I like Wendy a lot. More than a lot."

Will grinned. "You're in love with her."

"Yes."

"Have you told her?"

"No." He'd been afraid to admit his feelings, because they hadn't known each other long and he didn't want her to attribute his *I love you* to how well they got along in bed.

"How does Wendy feel about you?"

"I know she cares." And he believed she wouldn't have made love with him if her feelings for him hadn't been deeper than just *like*.

"So what's the problem?"

"Her parents."

Will's eyes widened.

Porter kicked a tennis ball lying in the driveway, and the sleeping Lab woke to bolt from his doghouse and chase after the toy. Tail wagging, he returned it to Porter and waited for him to throw it across the yard again.

"Go back to bed, Bandit." Porter tossed the ball in the direction of the doghouse. "Her parents don't think I'm good enough for their daughter."

"Then you have to prove them wrong."

"It's not that easy. I can't go put a new roof on her father's flower shop after a storm blows through."

Will stiffened.

"I didn't mean that as insult," Porter said. Will had won over Marsha's father after a storm had left a gaping hole in the pastor's church. Will and his friends had shown up the next day in force to repair the roof. "The problem is, I'm not Chinese and Wendy's parents want her to marry an Chinese man."

"Wendy's old enough to decide who she wants to marry, isn't she?"

"You'd think so." Porter walked a few steps away. "Like Marsha, Wendy's an only child and she's been raised to respect and please her parents."

"That means you not only have to prove to Wendy's parents that you're worthy of their daughter, but you have to convince Wendy that your love for her will help her get through the rough days ahead with her parents. If she decides to be with you, she has to know that you won't make her choose between them and you."

"But what if her parents disown her?"

"We'll be Wendy's family. She can claim the entire Cash clan as her family."

"You make it sound easy, but in your case Marsha didn't have to abandon her father because he accepted you. I don't think that's going to happen with me."

"You won't know unless you go for it."

"If Wendy picks me over her parents, it's bound to affect our relationship. I don't want her to wake up one morning resenting me because her parents no longer speak to her."

"There's always risk involved when you love someone."

"Yeah, but I can't change my ethnicity." Porter laughed, the harsh sound echoing in the dark. "I'm hardly an impressive candidate for son-in-law. I haul bulls to rodeos. Hell, Wendy makes twice the money I do."

"And Marsha makes more money teaching at the college than I do in construction," Will said. "It's not about the money or a successful career. It's about being a good man." Will pressed his fist to his chest. "It's about what's in here. Once you prove to Wendy's folks that you're the only man who can make their daughter happy, they'll see the light."

"I can't shake the feeling that no matter what I do, it won't be good enough."

"You won't know until you talk to them."

Will was right. He needed to ask Mr. Chin for his permission to marry his daughter. "I'll speak with Wendy's parents."

"Good." Will hopped into his truck then said, "If you ever need to talk…"

"Thanks, Will."

After his brother drove off, Porter stood in the dark for a long while, battling the panic in his gut. Confronting Wendy's parents would be the toughest thing he'd done to date—but he'd do anything for a shot at a future with Wendy.

"GOT A MINUTE?" Porter stood in the doorway of Buddy's office at Del Mar Ranch.

Buddy glanced up from the pile of papers on his desk and his eyes widened.

"Your housekeeper let me in." Porter had figured this meeting would be awkward, and judging from the beads of sweat popping out across his boss's brow, he was nervous, too.

"Sit down," Buddy said.

Porter took a seat in one of the matching leather chairs across from Buddy's desk. If he looked hard enough he might concede a slight resemblance to the older man. *Maybe.* Porter had rehearsed what he wanted to say on the way to the ranch, but now that he was face-to-face with Buddy, he couldn't remember a word. "Hank said you dated my mother."

Buddy's face turned bright red. "I did."

"And you think you're my father."

Buddy popped up from his chair and stared out the window facing the pasture. He remained silent, his posture rigid.

"It's not a big deal." Porter wanted to know the truth, but he refused to beg for information. He headed for the door.

"Wait, Porter." Buddy's shoulders slumped and he dragged a hand down his face as he turned from the window. "I dated your mother for a month." He cleared his throat. "And we slept together on the first date."

"My mother told you she was pregnant."

Buddy nodded. "She didn't specifically say that I was the father." He stared at his boots before looking Porter in the eye. "I should have demanded a paternity test."

"But you didn't."

"No, and I regret that."

"Why?"

"Because I've had to watch you from afar all these years, believing you were my son." Buddy cleared his throat. "Wanting to know the truth grew worse when I didn't have any kids of my own."

Porter wasn't sure how he felt about Buddy's admission. He admired the man for being honest, but it hurt knowing that his interest in Porter had grown out of not having any children.

Buddy returned to his desk and sank into the chair. "I'm not a hundred percent sure I'm your father, but there's a good chance that I am."

"Did you love my mother?"

"At the time I thought I did."

Porter felt bad for Buddy. It sucked loving a woman you couldn't be with. "After I was born did you confront my mother again?" According to Hank, Porter looked like Buddy. His boss must have noticed the similarities as Porter grew older.

"I went out to the pecan farm and offered to marry

your mother. She turned me down flat. A few weeks later when I stopped by, your grandmother said Aimee had taken off again and left you behind."

"Why didn't you ask my grandparents for a paternity test?"

"I was angry. And young. And hurt that Aimee didn't love me."

Porter understood. What young guy wanted to be saddled with the responsibility of raising a child while the mother—the woman he loved—flirted and slept with other men?

"What if I'm not your son?" Porter wasn't sure he was ready to face the truth. He'd convinced himself through the years that he didn't need a father—he had Johnny and his brothers to lean on. But deep down there had always been a yearning for the truth.

"I don't know." Buddy's mouth curved upward. He scratched his nose then his neck. "If it's okay with you, I'd like to take a paternity test and find out."

Caught off guard by the request, Porter didn't answer right away.

"A lot of years have gone by and you probably don't care anymore." Buddy cleared his throat. "But I'd like to know. I'd like to do right by you, if you are my son."

"You want to do right by me after twenty-eight years of standing aside and doing nothing?" The words escaped Porter's mouth before he could stop them. He cringed at losing his cool. "I'll think about it." He was halfway down the hall when he remembered Wendy.

He returned to Buddy's office and poked his head inside. "As my boss I need you to know that I had nothing to do with the bull that went missing after the King City rodeo."

"I didn't think you did."

"It's unusual how the bulls have all gone missing in a matter of months," Porter said.

Buddy narrowed his eyes. "Are you asking if I'm stealing my own livestock?"

"Are you?"

"No. And that's the God's honest truth."

Porter read the sincerity in Buddy's eyes and was relieved.

"If I don't find the bulls soon, my insurance company won't carry me anymore. I'll be too much of a liability."

Wendy hadn't mentioned dropping Buddy as a client. "I just needed to make sure."

"Porter?"

"What?"

"If you change your mind about the paternity test…"

"I'll let you know." Porter left the ranch and as he drove to the pecan farm he called himself every name in the book. He should have told Buddy to just go ahead and take the paternity test. But he'd been scared.

Scared of a positive test result.

Scared because it would change his life forever.

What if after getting to know Buddy better, he didn't like the man? Or he couldn't get over Buddy not trying to connect with him before now? Could he forgive the man and just move forward and forget the past? This whole are-you-my-father dilemma couldn't be happening at a worst time.

What he wanted more than anything—more than Buddy being his father—was Wendy.

Without Wendy, nothing mattered.

Chapter Thirteen

"What's wrong?" Wendy asked late Saturday afternoon at the rodeo in Deming. Porter paced next to the livestock truck, waiting his turn to load the two Del Mar bulls.

"Nothing."

Another curt response. Wendy couldn't help but assume Porter's agitation had to do with learning that Buddy might be his father, but she also attributed some of his unease to her ending their relationship. After being lectured all week about duty and responsibility, she was more convinced than ever that marriage with any man her parents didn't approve of would fail. But no matter how much Porter resented her for not having the courage to defy her mother and father, it didn't change how she felt about him.

She'd fallen in love with Porter Wagoner Cash.

"Have you had a chance to speak with Buddy since Hank shared his suspicions with you?" she asked.

"Yeah." Porter didn't make eye contact. "Buddy's not rustling his livestock."

"You asked him that?"

"Yep."

"And you believe he's telling the truth?"

"I do." Porter finally looked at her. "He suspects you'll drop his coverage after you pay the insurance claims."

Carl had spoken to Wendy about the situation, warning her that she might have to cancel Buddy's policy. That was one phone call she wasn't looking forward to making. "Buddy's been my client since I began with American Livestock and I'm doing everything I can to find out the truth." She spread her arms wide. "Why do you think I'm here? I don't want Del Mar Rodeo to go under."

"Hey, Cash!" A cowboy signaled from across the lot. "You're next."

"I'll wait in the car while they load the bulls," she said.

"If you lose sight of the trailer in traffic, we're heading south on Route 11 to Sunshine."

"I put it in the GPS."

Porter hopped into the truck then backed it up to the bull pen. Clipboard in hand, he checked the identification of the two bulls before the rodeo helpers escorted them inside the trailer. Wendy walked across the lot to her car. The drive from Deming to the Kennedys' ranch near the town of Sunshine was an hour. Hopefully the map dot boasted a decent restaurant so she and Porter could grab dinner and talk—although she expected he'd have nothing to say.

The car was hotter than Hades after sitting in the sun all day. While she waited for the air-conditioning to cool the interior, she noticed a man loitering near the bull pens, texting on his phone. He checked over his shoulder every few seconds, as if worried he was being watched.

She kept her eye on the guy—since investigating Buddy's missing bulls she'd become suspicious of everyone. Ten minutes passed before Porter secured the trailer door and drove away from the pens. Wendy slid behind the wheel, then checked the rearview mirror before backing up. She hit the brakes when the loitering man got into a Ford truck with heavy front-end damage and a horse trailer attached to the back. The man gunned the engine then pulled out behind Porter as he passed by.

Wendy followed at a distance, but not too far that she didn't notice the pickup had no license plate. She hoped it was just a coincidence, but intuition insisted the man in the Ford was up to no good. Wendy grabbed her cell phone and hit five—she'd added Porter's number to her speed dial when she'd accompanied him to Colorado.

"What's up?"

"You're being followed," she said.

"You mean the blue Ford that's towing a horse trailer?"

"I saw the guy watch you load the bulls back at the fairgrounds. As soon as you backed away, he got into his pickup and followed you out of the fairgrounds." She eased up on the accelerator when the truck in front of her slowed down. "And Porter…"

"What?"

"There's no license plate on the vehicle."

"I'll keep an eye on him. Thanks for letting me know."

"Maybe you should gas up and see if he stops, too."

"The ranch isn't that far. I'd rather keep going." He disconnected the call.

Twenty-five minutes later, Porter signaled and turned

onto a gravel path then drove beneath tall pine arches with the words *Kennedy Ranch* burned into the wood. The beat-up Ford sped past the entrance, and Wendy breathed a sigh of relief—false alarm. She trailed Porter for a half mile before a sea of barns and corrals came into view.

He parked by the largest corral, and she pulled up next to him.

"Looks like the guy took off," Porter said when she got out of her car.

"I sure didn't like the way he acted." The man's scruffy face had been half hidden beneath his cowboy hat, which he'd tipped forward, as if trying to conceal his identity.

"Howdy, folks!" A man with snow-white hair walked toward them.

"Porter Cash." Porter shook hands with the cowboy. "I've got two Del Mar rodeo bulls that need a rest."

"Stan Kennedy. Welcome to my ranch." The older man's blue eyes twinkled when he shifted his gaze to Wendy. "Is this your partner?"

She shook Stan's hand. "I'm Wendy Chin. I work for American Livestock Insurance. Buddy Davidson is my client."

"Buddy phoned last week and told me he'd lost a few bulls." Stan's brow furrowed. "I'd trust my ranch hands with my life. His livestock will be safe on my property."

"Where should I unload them?" Porter asked.

"I've got a pasture all fenced in and ready for them." Stan pointed to the gravel path they'd just driven. "Go back the way you came but take the fork in the road. Drive a quarter mile and you'll see the pasture. There's a stock tank with fresh water, the grass is good and I've got feeders out there, too."

"I'll get the paperwork." Porter retrieved the forms from the truck, and Stan signed them.

"You two are welcome to come up to the house for coffee after you unload the bulls."

"Thanks, but we need to head back to Yuma." Wendy ignored Porter's questioning glance.

"Drive carefully." Stan tipped his hat and walked off.

Wendy followed the livestock truck along the gravel path. Five minutes later they arrived at the pasture, but she remained in the car while Porter released the bulls. The animals walked straight to the water tank and drank, then moseyed over to the feeder to sniff the food. Porter removed the extra hay from the trailer and dropped it inside the fence, then stowed the ramp and shut the doors.

When he approached the driver's side of her car, she lowered the window. "There's a diner thirty minutes from here where we can eat if you're hungry," he said.

"Sounds good." Wendy watched him double-check that the pasture gate had been locked then get into the truck and head for the highway.

As they drove off she glanced in the rearview mirror and gasped. A pickup towing a horse trailer sped through the pasture toward the bulls. It was the banged-up Ford that had followed Porter out of the Deming fairgrounds. Wendy reached for her cell phone again.

"He's back."

"Who?"

"The pickup with the missing license plate."

Porter hit the brakes, and Wendy did the same. "I'm

turning around. Call the sheriff's department and Kennedy," he said.

Wendy pulled over, then dialed 911 while keeping an eye on the Ford. The driver got out of his vehicle and opened the doors on the horse trailer.

"Nine-one-one. What's your emergency?"

After being assured that a sheriff's deputy had been dispatched to the location, she called Stan Kennedy, but was forced to leave a voice mail message.

Porter was having trouble repositioning the livestock trailer on the narrow path, and she was concerned that if she didn't distract the thief, he'd get away with the bulls, so she laid on the car horn.

The man looked her way once but ignored her and grabbed a rope from the bed of the pickup. He approached one of the bulls cautiously and lassoed the animal after only two tries. Wendy blasted the horn again, and he flashed his middle finger as he led the bull into the trailer.

Porter had managed to turn the truck around and was gaining speed as he passed Wendy's car. He blew his horn but the loud noise did nothing to deter the thief from trying to catch the second bull, which trotted off when the rope flew his way. Porter reached the pasture but the fence cut him off from the other truck. He jumped out of the cab and entered the meadow.

Be careful, Porter.

When the thief saw Porter, he abandoned his attempt to capture the second bull and raced for his pickup. Too late. A pair of patrol cars, sirens blaring, approached from the east, cutting off the escape route.

The thief ran, but the deputies closed in on him. The man stumbled and pitched forward, falling to the ground. The officers stopped their vehicles and hopped out, guns drawn. The man didn't resist arrest and the deputies cuffed him, then put him in the back of a patrol car.

Wendy left her car and watched Porter unload the bull from the horse trailer. Once the animals were back where they belonged, he joined her, and they waited for the deputies to speak with them.

"Do you know who the guy is?" Porter asked the lawman.

"He's not talking to us and he had no ID on him. It'll be a while before we find out his name."

"He followed us from the Deming fairgrounds earlier in the day," Wendy said.

The deputy opened a notebook. "I'll take down your statements, then you're free to go."

Porter spoke with the officer for five minutes, then the deputy returned to his squad car and drove off.

"Maybe now we'll find out who's been stealing Del Mar's livestock," Wendy said.

Porter tucked a loose strand of hair behind her ear, and she shivered at the intimate touch. "Are you okay?"

As she gazed into his brown eyes, she saw all the love she'd ever need the rest of her life. "Porter."

"What?"

"Just this." She stood on tiptoe and kissed him. She couldn't say the words, but she wanted to show him how much she loved him. A honking horn interrupted their intimate embrace, and they broke apart.

"I think that's Kennedy," Porter said.

"I'll call my boss and give him an update." Wendy returned to her car and phoned Carl. The conversation lasted ten minutes. When she ended the call she no-

ticed Porter was watching her. The yearning in his gaze
brought tears to her eyes. Tears from losing a love that
only came along once in a lifetime.

SUNDAY AFTERNOON PORTER sat on his bed in the bunkhouse staring at two $25,000 money orders. It turned
out Buddy Davidson had posted a $50,000 reward for
any information leading to the apprehension of those
responsible for rustling his cattle. Buddy had split the
money between Porter and Wendy. And Wendy had
mailed Porter her share of the reward money along with
a note.

> Dear Porter,
> I want to wake up every day knowing that you
> made your dream come true at the Morning Sun-
> shine Ranch.
> Wendy

Didn't she know his dream had changed? What good
would it do to own a ranch if he didn't have Wendy to
share it with? He'd rather work a ten-hour shift seven
days a week on an assembly line if it allowed him to
come home to Wendy at the end of the day.

Make it happen.

He'd skated through life, his brothers giving him a
pass because he was the youngest of the boys. He'd re-
lied on Johnny to fix the things he'd broken, stand up
for him at school when kids mocked his name and in-
tervene with their grandparents when they'd wanted to
discipline him. Now it was Porter's turn to step up and
manage his own affairs.

He loved Wendy. And he needed her in his life.

The only way he had a chance of being with her was if he convinced her parents that their daughter's happiness was more important than their agenda or his ethnicity. He stuffed the money orders into his wallet, then checked his reflection in the mirror before grabbing his Stetson and leaving the bunkhouse.

He had no idea what to say to Wendy's parents but he'd think of something during the drive into Yuma.

Thirty minutes later he pulled into a parking space in front of the flower shop and cut the engine. His stomach was tied in knots, and his heart beat like a jackhammer. The business hours in the window read eleven to five on Sundays. It was only ten, but he suspected the Chins were already hard at work. He removed his cowboy hat and set it on the seat, then got out.

He knocked and held his breath, waiting to see if they'd ignore him. A full minute later, Wendy's father opened the door and greeted Porter with a cool "Good morning."

"Mr. Chin, do you have a moment? I'd like to speak to you about your daughter." After Porter entered the store, Wendy's father flipped the lock.

He faced the older man—only fifteen feet separated them but the differences in their cultures made the distance feel as wide as an ocean. He opened his mouth to speak, but Wendy's mother entered the room.

"I can't find the flower shears I bought last week. Do you—" She froze when she saw Porter.

"Good morning, Mrs. Chin. I hope you don't mind me stopping by before you open for the day. I wanted to speak with both of you about my feelings for Wendy."

Face pale, Mrs. Chin inched closer to her husband.

"I came here to tell you that I love your daughter.

She's an amazing woman, and I know you're very proud of her." He paused, hoping one of them would speak, but they stood stone-faced.

"I don't know what you've heard about me or my family." He shrugged. "I can't change who I am, but I promise to treat your daughter with respect and honor her not only with my words but my actions, as well."

"What is he asking?" Mrs. Chin whispered to her husband.

"I believe he wants to marry our daughter."

She slapped a hand over her heart and gawked at Porter.

Not the reaction he'd hoped for. "Have you already proposed to Wendy?" Mr. Chin asked.

"No." He hadn't even bought a ring. "I was hoping to get your blessing first."

"Wendy is our only child. We want what's best for her."

"I understand, sir. But if you'll give me a chance, I'll prove to you that I can make Wendy happy."

"How will you provide for her?"

Porter broke out in a sweat. "I plan to start up a rodeo contracting business." Mr. Chin's eyes sparked with interest, and Porter rushed on. "I've got my eye on a ranch in the Fortuna Foothills."

"Do you have the money to buy that ranch?" he asked.

"Not yet, sir."

Mr. Chin turned his back to Porter and stared out the window. "You're asking me to hand over my daughter's future to you when your own future is uncertain. What about Wendy's career?"

"I won't make any decisions without Wendy's approval." Why were her parents so focused on goals, careers and income? What happened to just wanting their daughter to be happy?

The older couple exchanged glances. They didn't have to bring up the subject—he knew what they were thinking. The job issue aside, Wendy was Chinese and Porter was not. "I can't change my ethnicity," he said. "But love doesn't pay any attention to race or socio-economic status."

The somber stare Mr. Chin leveled at Porter spoke volumes, and he knew in his gut that he'd lost this round. "I love your daughter and I want to marry her. But I won't propose to her unless I have your blessing because whether you realize it or not, Wendy loves and respects you both very much. So much that she's willing to sacrifice her own happiness just to please you."

Porter left the store and drove out of town. Before he realized how far he'd gone, he was halfway to Buddy's ranch. He pulled onto the shoulder and shifted the pickup into Park. What was he doing?

He stared out the windshield, trying to come to terms with his conversation with Wendy's parents and his instinctive reaction to seek out advice from his… Shoot, he didn't know yet if Buddy was his biological father or not. Porter wasn't even sure he wanted to know the truth.

The truth would force him to sort through the baggage he'd kept locked inside him all these years. Sure, a part of him would always want to know who his father was, but now that he'd fallen in love with Wendy, he didn't feel that driving need anymore. He just wanted to focus on finding a way to be with Wendy—that was what was most important.

Porter merged with traffic and drove the rest of the way to the ranch. When he arrived, Buddy was studying a bull in the corral closest to the barn.

"This is a nice surprise," Buddy said. "Did you make a decision on whether or not you want me to take a paternity test?"

"I'm not sure I'm ready to learn if you're my father." The disappointment on Buddy's face socked Porter in the gut. "If you are, it changes everything between me and my brothers."

"How's that?"

"None of their fathers wanted anything to do with them. I'd be the only brother who had a relationship with his father."

"And that's a bad thing?"

"No, it's just that it's been me and my brothers all of our lives, and Johnny's always been the one I turned to when I needed advice or help."

Buddy put his hand on Porter's shoulder and squeezed. "You don't have to do anything right now, or ever, if you don't want to. It was selfish of me to come forward after all these years and throw this in your lap." He rubbed his brow. "But I've felt so damned guilty because I didn't demand the truth from your mother."

"Why didn't you?"

"I wanted to inherit this ranch. My grandfather and his father before him worked their backsides off to get Del Mar Rodeo Productions on the map and I wanted to continue the tradition."

"Why couldn't you have done that even if I was your son?"

"Your mother had a wild reputation, Porter. My folks were God-fearing people and they would have dis-

owned me if I'd married your mother or claimed you."
He cleared his throat. "When your mother turned down
my offer to marry her after she told me she was pregnant, I was relieved that I was off the hook." He pressed
his hand to his heart. "It's not something I'm proud of,
but it's the truth."

"I appreciate your honesty." As a matter of fact, Porter felt better about the situation.

"As the years passed by I felt more and more selfish for choosing my inheritance over being your father.
Once my folks passed on and this—" Buddy spread his
arms wide "—became mine, I considered contacting
you but chickened out, figuring you'd want nothing to
do with me."

"I probably wouldn't have," Porter said.

"And then I got married and we were trying to start
a family, but Cathy had several miscarriages. Ten years
of failed pregnancies took a toll on our marriage and
we divorced."

"I'm sorry."

"Cathy remarried and she's happy now. I'm glad for
her. But all those years we were together I kept thinking in the back of my mind that I had a son already, but
I couldn't claim him."

Porter opened his mouth to remind him they didn't
know for sure they were related, but Buddy cut him off.
"I don't need a test to tell me you're my son, Porter. This
may sound crazy, but in my heart you've been my son
since you were born. I've felt a connection with you for
years—I was just a foolish, scared man and didn't do
anything about it. So it doesn't matter to me if we ever
find out the truth. I'll still consider you mine."

Porter was humbled by Buddy's confession.

"The ball's in your court. I won't push you, but I want you to know I'm here for you as a father, not just a boss."

Porter felt a tiny crack near his heart after listening to Buddy. Maybe it wouldn't hurt to open up to him. "I'm in love with Wendy Chin and I want to marry her."

"Congratulations. She's a fine woman." Buddy grinned. "Have you proposed yet?"

"No." Porter looked down at his boots. "It's complicated."

"I've got all day."

Porter's chest tightened. That was something a parent would say to their child. "Wendy's father wants her to marry a man of his choosing. Culture and tradition are very important to them."

"Are they important to Wendy?"

"Yes and no. She feels a need to please her parents."

"I'm guessing Wendy won't marry you unless she has her parents' blessing."

"I can't change my ethnicity, and all they know about me is what they've heard through the grapevine about the Cash brothers." He scuffed his boot against the rail. "I doubt it was complimentary."

"Then you have to change their minds about you."

"That won't be easy when they think I have nothing to offer Wendy except my love." He expelled a harsh breath. "It's not like I don't have a plan for the future. I've got my eye on a ranch in the Fortuna Foothills. I've been saving money toward a down payment but it's going to take—"

"That ranch wouldn't happen to be called Morning Sunshine, would it?"

"That's the one. What do you know about the place?"

"Not much except that it's been vacant for so long it'd take a lot of money to bring it back to life again."

Porter hadn't considered what type of investment he'd need to update the place. He'd only focused on buying it. "How much money?"

"Depends on what you have planned for the property."

"I was thinking of raising bucking stock." Porter squared his shoulders. "I had the idea before I found out you might be my father."

Buddy got a thoughtful look on his face. "I've mostly dealt with rodeo bulls because that's where the big money is, but with all the trouble I've had lately I've thought of adding bucking horses to the mix." Then Buddy surprised Porter with his next question. "Do you believe Wendy's parents will look at you differently if you own a ranch and run your own business?"

"I hope they would."

"Have you considered taking on a business partner?"

If Buddy partnered with Porter, the bank would surely loan them the money for improvements. For the first time since Porter left the flower shop, he felt hopeful. "I would if the terms were right."

"Let me speak with my lawyer and I'll get back to you."

"You don't have to do this."

"Do what?"

"Help me just because you feel bad that... You know."

"I'll always feel bad I didn't step forward before now. That will never change. But this would be a business deal, plain and simple. How much do you have to put down on the property?"

"Fifty thousand. Wendy gave me her share of the reward money, but I don't feel right about taking it from you or her."

"You two saved my business. You earned it fair and square." Buddy's phone went off, and he checked the number. "I've got to take this. I'll be in touch soon."

Porter drove off trying to make sense of what had just happened between Buddy and himself. Deep down he knew the truth—he and Buddy were related—but he wanted his brothers to know first that he intended to ask Buddy to take a paternity test.

In truth he'd give up knowing who his father was and owning a ranch in a heartbeat if he could be with Wendy for the rest of his life. Winning the Chins' approval would take hard work and time, but he was willing to do anything to prove he was the right man for their daughter.

Chapter Fourteen

After work on Thursday Wendy drove to the flower shop. She'd finally gotten up the courage to tell her parents they were wrong—they didn't know what was best for her. They'd told her that Porter had paid them a visit but had refused to share any details about the conversation, only reiterating that they believed he wasn't the right man for her.

But he was.

Wendy had done a lot of soul-searching the past few weeks and she'd finally owned up to the truth—she'd pushed Porter away not to honor her parents' wishes but because of fear. Tyler's betrayal had left her afraid to commit her heart to another man, and she'd used her parents' disapproval of Porter as an excuse to push him away. Porter might not be the man her parents wished for her, but her heart insisted she'd be a fool not to trust in his love for her...in their love for each other.

And the crazy thing was that neither of them had said the words out loud. There had been no need for declarations. Their love for each other showed in every glance, every touch and every word.

She left the car and entered the shop through the back door, then stopped suddenly when she heard a deep baritone voice coming from the front of the store. She peeked past the doorway and spotted her parents behind the counter, facing off with Buddy Davidson.

"I want you both to know how much I appreciate having your daughter as my insurance agent. She went above and beyond her job description to help track down the culprits who stole my bulls. The sheriff stopped by my ranch today and told me that my manager, Hank Martin, was behind the rustling." Buddy shook his head. "Thanks to Wendy's persistence, he won't be stealing any more bulls from me."

Wendy had received a text from Carl that morning, telling her that Martin had confessed to being the mastermind behind stealing the Del Mar bulls. She hadn't wanted to tell Porter the news until after she'd settled things with her parents.

"You should be proud of your daughter," Buddy said. "She's a bright, savvy businesswoman, not to mention she's the love of Porter Cash's life."

Wendy drew in a quick breath, surprised Porter had told Buddy about their relationship.

"I came here today to vouch for Porter and assure you that his intentions toward your daughter are honorable." Buddy waved a hand before his face. "It's a long story that goes back a lot of years, but I had a relationship with Porter's mother and…I've always thought of him as my own." Buddy cleared his throat.

"Porter's grandparents Ely and Ada Cash did a fine job raising him and the rest of the Cash boys. He may not be who you had in mind for your daughter, but he'll love Wendy and stand by her through good and bad."

Wendy's father opened his mouth to respond, but

Buddy shook his head. "You don't have to say anything. I just wanted you to know that your daughter picked a fine young man to fall in love with."

The bells on the door jingled but Wendy remained in the shadows unable to see who'd entered the store. "Hello, Mr. and Mrs. Chin. I'm Johnny Cash, Porter's eldest brother."

Good grief, what is going on?

"Nice to see you, Johnny," Buddy said. "I stopped by to speak to Wendy's parents on Porter's behalf."

"What do you know? I'm here for the same reason."

Wendy peeked around the doorjamb. Her parents' shocked faces were comical.

"Mr. and Mrs. Chin, my brother mentioned that you had concerns about him marrying Wendy. I can vouch for Porter that he'll honor your Chinese heritage and make you both proud of him."

The bells jingled again, and Wendy's eyes widened when the remaining Cash brothers filed into the shop.

"Figures you'd beat us to the punch," Will said. He nodded to Wendy's parents. "Mr. and Mrs. Chin, I'm Will Cash and these are my brothers—" he pointed to each "—Mack, Conway and Buck."

Tears welled in Wendy's eyes. Buck had driven all the way from Lizard Gulch to show his support for Porter. Couldn't her parents see how amazing the Cash family was?

"We're here to tell you that Porter is an honorable man with integrity and—"

"I covered all that," Johnny interrupted Buck.

"Did you tell them that Porter's not the goof-off people think he is?" Mack asked.

"And even though Porter hasn't held a job for very

long until he started hauling roughstock for Buddy," Will said, "he's serious about his future and ready to settle down."

"And you assured them that Porter will support Wendy no matter if he has to hold down two jobs," Conway said.

The bells jingled again, and Dixie entered. "What are you guys doing here?" She glanced at each brother then turned her smile on Wendy's parents. "Hi, Mr. and Mrs. Chin. Don't let my brothers scare you. They're harmless." She approached the counter and spoke to the group. "Does Porter know you're here?"

A chorus of nos rang out.

Dixie turned to Wendy's parents. "Your daughter and I have been friends since junior high and to be honest, when I first heard that Porter liked Wendy, I threw a hissy fit. I know you want Wendy to marry a Chinese man, but there's no man anywhere in the world who will love her as much as Porter does."

"We already told them that, Dix," Conway said.

She ignored her brother and continued talking. "Wendy admires you both so much and it's because of you two that she succeeds at everything she does. You've taught her the meaning of hard work. Marrying my brother isn't going to erase any of that."

Wendy's parents still hadn't spoken a word when the door opened again and Marsha Cash pushed her father's wheelchair into the store. "Oh, my," she said. "I wasn't expecting a crowd."

"Mr. and Mrs. Chin, this is my wife, Marsha," Will said. "And my father-in-law, Pastor Bugler."

"When I heard that you didn't approve of Porter," Pastor Bugler said, "I wanted to speak on his behalf."

Wendy's parents still looked shell-shocked.

"A daughter is priceless and special, and not so long ago I believed William Cash was no good for Marsha. It's difficult to trust another man to look after your daughter." The pastor grasped Marsha's hand. "Not until I understood that my objection to William had to do with my fear of losing my daughter was I able to give him a chance to prove me wrong." The pastor nodded to Will. "I couldn't ask for a better son-in-law. If you give Porter a chance, he'll prove you wrong, too. The Cash brothers are solid, steady men who put their wives and families first."

"I'll vouch for that." Shannon and her father walked through the door. "Hello, Mr. and Mrs. Chin," she said. "Looks like we all had the same idea." She tugged her father through the crowd and stopped next to Dixie by the register. "My father will swear an oath that Porter is a good man."

"I've had the pleasure of employing the Cash men through the years," Mr. Douglas said. "They've been a big help to me during spring roundup. Of all the brothers who helped out at my ranch, it was Porter who kept the hands in good spirits. Branding is tiring work and when the men complained, Porter knew how to tease them into a good mood."

Mr. Douglas made eye contact with Johnny, then said, "Life has its ups and downs for every couple, and the Cash brothers are true blue to the bone. Porter makes this family laugh and reminds them to stop and smell the roses along the trail."

Wendy pressed her fingers to her trembling lips. What Shannon's father said was true—Porter made her smile and he showed her how to have fun.

"We've all said our piece." Johnny nodded to Wendy's parents. "Thank you for listening, Mr. and Mrs. Chin." He left the store first, and the others followed, leaving her parents dazed.

Wendy wiped the last of her tears away and abandoned her hiding place. Her mother gasped when she spotted Wendy. "How long were you eavesdropping?"

"Long enough to hear everything," she said.

"Wendy." Her father frowned. "I'm impressed that all those people came here today to speak on Porter's behalf."

Hope bloomed in Wendy's heart, then died a slow death with her father's next words.

"But regardless of who vouches for him, nothing will change the fact that Porter is not Chinese. I can't condone a marriage between you two."

A lump formed in Wendy's throat, but she swallowed hard and straightened her shoulders. "I'm sorry you feel that way, Dad. Everything I've done in my life has been to please you and Mom. I've been an obedient daughter and I've followed your wishes in almost every decision I've made. But I can't do it anymore. Not if I have to give up the one man who will make me happy. Not if I have to give up the man I want to grow old with."

Her mother's mouth dropped open.

"I'm marrying Porter. He's the man *I* choose to build a life and a family with. The man *I* know will make you both proud, if you give him a chance." She drew in a deep breath. "Mom, when Dad watches you arrange flowers, I see his love for you in his eyes. And when you talk about Dad, I hear that same love in your voice. I want that, too. And I can have that with Porter."

"But you have nothing in common with him," her father protested. "He won't be a good provider."

"You believe only Chinese men are dedicated to their careers and will provide for their families. Porter works just as hard if not harder than the men you've introduced me to." Tears welled in her eyes. "You can't always measure success and security by a paycheck or a promotion, Dad." Wendy didn't wait for her parents to respond. She left the shop, her chest aching so badly it hurt to draw in a deep breath. Eyes burning, she drove off.

Don't lose faith. They'll come around.

She prayed she was right, because if her parents disowned her, she'd really need Porter's smile to mend her shattered heart. Next on her to-do list was buying wedding rings and arranging a ceremony, and who better to help her with that task than her future sisters-in-law?

PORTER SAT IN a booth at a diner outside of Yuma on Thursday morning and waited for Buddy. He was ready to give his okay for Buddy to take a paternity test. He'd spoken to his brothers and they'd assured him that they'd always be there no matter what and that Porter deserved a shot at having a real father-son relationship.

Taking this next step with Buddy should have given Porter a sense of relief and anticipation, but instead he felt depressed. He couldn't recall experiencing such emptiness—a bottomless pit in his gut that had *Wendy* written all over it.

The restaurant door opened, and Buddy walked in. When he saw Porter, he waved. Coffeepot in hand, the waitress followed him and filled Buddy's cup as soon as he sat down across from Porter.

"Thank you," Buddy said.

"You two know what you want?" The middle-aged redhead pulled a pencil from behind her ear and tapped the lead against her order pad.

"I'll take the grand slam," Porter said. "Scrambled. Bacon. Wheat toast."

"I'll have the same." Buddy slid the menu back in place between the ketchup and mustard bottles.

"Comin' right up."

After the waitress walked off, Buddy said, "Not sure if you'd heard, but Hank Martin was arrested for rustling my bulls."

That was the big news. "You two were friends for a long while."

"I thought we were." Buddy stared out the window next to their booth. "He had gambling problem and was in deep with his bookie. He said he felt guilty about stealing from me, but it didn't stop him." Buddy sipped his coffee then grinned. "I'm hoping you asked to meet for breakfast because you came to a decision."

Porter nodded. "I have. I'd like you to go ahead and take the paternity test."

"I'll call my doctor's office and see what I need to do."

Porter was relieved Buddy didn't make a big issue out of the request.

The waitress arrived with their food and topped off their coffee cups, then they dug in, neither speaking until they'd finished their meals. "What happens to Hank now?" Porter asked.

"He'll do prison time. He gave up the names of everyone involved in the cattle-rustling ring. They were stealing bulls from other ranches in Montana and Idaho."

"Where were they shipping the roughstock?"

"Canada."

"I bet Wendy's happy to have the case solved."

Buddy studied Porter. "When did you last talk to her?"

"It's been a while." Too long. "Why?"

"I probably shouldn't have done it, but I felt compelled to speak on your behalf to Wendy's folks."

"When?"

"I went by the flower shop two weeks ago." He rubbed a hand over his jaw. "I wasn't the only one who came to your defense."

Porter's eyes widened.

"Your brothers stopped in along with Will's wife and Pastor Bugler. Then Shannon and her father showed up. You had an army of supporters testifying on your behalf."

Porter's throat grew thick. "I didn't know." His siblings hadn't said a word to him.

"You have a mighty fine family, Porter."

"I do." Now if only he could make Mr. and Mrs. Chin see that his family would provide all the love and support he and Wendy would ever need.

"You mind if I ask where things stand between you and Wendy?"

"It's complicated." Porter didn't want to admit he'd contemplated throwing in the towel and walking away for Wendy's sake, but his love for her wouldn't let him. Not yet. "I just have to figure out how to get past her parents."

"Don't give up," Buddy said.

Porter wasn't calling it quits. He was planning phase two of his campaign to win over Wendy's parents. He'd met with the bank and they'd taken his fifty thousand as down payment on Morning Sunshine Ranch, then approved a loan to finance the rest.

"I'm glad you want me to take that paternity test, Porter, and no matter which way it comes out I'd still like to partner up with you if you decide to buy the ranch in the foothills."

"I bought the place last week, thanks to the fifty thousand from your reward money."

"I hope you won't get mad about this." Buddy stuck a finger inside his shirt collar and scratched his neck. "But I got a couple of leads on some good bucking horses."

"Buddy—"

"Hear me out." He raised a hand in protest. "I know it will take a while to put up corrals and invest in the infrastructure needed to raise bucking horses, but we could keep the pair at Del Mar until you're ready for them at Morning Sunshine."

"I don't have the money to buy horses right now."

"I do. Offering to be your business partner won't make up for twenty-eight years of not having a father, but it's the least I can do to show you that my intentions are sincere."

Buddy didn't need to prove anything to Porter. "Where are these horses you like?"

"One's up in Wyoming and the other is in Oklahoma."

Porter's chest tightened. "We don't even know yet if you're my father."

"Doesn't matter. This is a business decision. I've got

the capital to purchase bucking horses, but I don't have the space at my ranch to keep them long-term."

Buddy was handing Porter his dream—a way to provide for Wendy and prove to her parents that he was serious about a future with their daughter. And until they could afford to build a proper home at Morning Sunshine, he and Wendy could live in her apartment. He was certain her parents would approve of that.

"Well," Porter said, smiling. "I've got the land but I don't have the horses."

"Then it looks like we need each other," Buddy said.

"I guess it does." Porter held out his hand and they shook on the deal.

"Maybe you and Wendy could spend your honeymoon up there in Wyoming and check out that horse."

"I have to propose to her first," Porter said.

"Don't take too long. Someone's bound to snatch up those broncs soon."

"Buddy," Porter said, "I don't want to let you down."

"You were meant to be in the ranching business. It's in your blood." Buddy grabbed the check the waitress set on the table as she walked by. "I'm paying."

"The next one's on me."

"I'll hold you to that." Buddy slid from the booth.

A feeling of rightness filled Porter when they stood to say goodbye. Buddy surprised him by pulling him close for a bear hug before leaving the diner.

Porter sat back down and finished his coffee. He'd been avoiding his brothers, not wanting to field questions about him and Wendy. But after hearing his siblings had stepped up on his behalf, he owed them a thank-you.

Then he'd phone Dixie and ask for her help in planning a romantic proposal that Wendy couldn't say no to.

WENDY PACED ACROSS the rug inside the bunkhouse at the Cash farm. She'd never been this nervous about anything in her life. The sound of a truck engine met her ears, and she hurried to the window.

Porter.

The butterflies in her stomach took flight and she felt nauseous. She checked the sofa table, making sure everything looked perfect—the expensive bottle of red wine and crystal glasses. The two gift-wrapped boxes with silver bows.

The door to the bunkhouse opened, and Porter stepped inside. He turned his back to her as he set his hat on the counter. Then he stiffened. "Wendy?"

Her heart thudded inside her chest. "It's me."

He faced her and smiled. "I thought I smelled your perfume." His stare bored into her. "You're a difficult lady to get a hold of."

"I've been doing a lot of thinking." *And planning.*

"Thinking about what?"

"You. Me. The future." *Our future.*

He closed the gap between them and clasped her hands. "What's all this?" He nodded to the items on the table.

"I've never done anything like this before, so I'm a little nervous." She flashed a shaky smile. "I want this to be special."

"Want what to be special?"

She picked up a gift box. "This is for you."

"You bought me a gift?"

"Open it."

His big fingers fumbled with the wrapping paper, then his gaze clashed with hers.

"I love you, Porter Cash, and I deserve you. No one is going to tell me that I can't be with you."

He opened the box and stared at the silver wedding band. "Are you asking what I think you're asking?"

"Will you marry me, Porter?"

"What'd he say?" A loud whisper drifted through the open window behind Wendy.

"Shut up, Mack. He hasn't answered yet."

"Maybe he didn't understand the question, Conway."

"If you'd quit talking we might hear something."

Wendy ignored the brothers and focused on Porter.

"What about your parents?" he asked.

"I'd do anything for them, but I'm not willing to sacrifice my love for you. My parents want me to be happy and eventually they'll see how perfect you are for me."

"What if they don't?"

"Then I still choose you," she said. "I can't imagine not sharing my life with you."

"I don't have a ring for you."

"Yes, you do." She handed him the other jeweler's box.

He grinned. "Did I pick out a good one?"

Eyes burning, she said, "Oh, yeah. This will put you in debt for a while."

"Guess I better see what I spent my hard-earned money on." He unwrapped the box and opened the lid, revealing a princess-cut solitaire diamond. "I have good taste."

"I want only the best. That's why I want you."

"Hey, that was good line." A loud *oomph* sounded outside the window.

Porter removed the diamond and held her left hand. "Wendy Chin, will you do me the honor of becoming my wife?"

Tears of joy ran down her cheeks. "Yes, I will." He slid the ring onto her finger and pulled her into his arms.

"They're kissing now."

When they came up for air, Porter called out. "I said yes, you idiots! Now beat it so I can make love to my fiancée!"

"We're out of here," Conway's voice rang out.

"Porter, are you sure?" Wendy asked.

"I've been in love with you since I rescued you from the bathroom at the gas station and found you sitting on the toilet tank texting on your phone."

She rose on tiptoe and brought her mouth closer to his. "I hope you don't mind, but I took the liberty of planning our wedding, because I want us to be man and wife as soon as possible."

He hugged her close. "You're my forever girl, Wendy."

"And I finally have a cowboy of my own."

Porter kissed her long, slow and deep before coming up for air. "When does our wedding take place?"

"Tomorrow."

Porter beamed. "Does everyone know about this already?"

"Yes. Dixie helped me plan the ceremony and Marsha, Shannon, Isi, Beth and Destiny worked on the decorations and making sure the invitations got sent to everyone."

"Did Buddy get invited?"

"He did."

"He gave us our wedding present early," Porter said.

"What wedding present?"

Porter took her hand and tugged her down to the couch, then nestled her in his lap. "I met with Buddy before coming here and told him that I'd bought Morning Sunshine Ranch."

Wendy gasped. "Are you serious? You own the ranch?"

"No, *we* own the ranch. I used all of the reward money as a down payment and financed the rest."

Wendy buried her face against his neck and groaned. "Don't tell me we have to spend our honeymoon in that awful trailer."

"If Buddy has his way we'll be honeymooning in Wyoming."

"Wyoming?"

"Buddy's my new business partner. He's investing in bucking horses that we're going to raise at Morning Sunshine."

"Sounds like the two of you have made your peace."

"I asked him to take a paternity test."

Wendy hugged Porter hard. She sensed how badly he wanted the test to turn out positive. For his sake, she hoped Buddy was his biological father.

"No matter the results," Porter said, "we'll be fine. Buddy says it's too late not to think of me as his son after believing I've been his all along."

"I'm happy for you."

"We're going to have a good life, Wendy. I promise."

"I'll hold you to that promise, cowboy." She snuggled deeper into his embrace. She'd need Porter's love and support if her parents never accepted him or their marriage. She shoved the thought to the back of her mind, not wanting to ruin this special moment.

"Wendy?"

"What?"

Porter kissed her as he pressed her down on the couch. "Tomorrow can't come soon enough."

Epilogue

"I can't believe Wendy planned this wedding in less than two weeks," Porter said, yanking on his bow tie.

Johnny swatted Porter's hand away and straightened the tie.

"Is it bad luck to think of another woman on your wedding day?" Porter stared at his brothers, gathered in the room outside the chapel of the Mission Community Church, where Pastor Bugler would marry him and Wendy.

"You having second thoughts?" Buck asked.

"No. I just woke up this morning thinking about Veronica Patriot and—" His brothers exchanged nervous glances. "Whoa. It's not like that."

"Then what is it like?" Mack asked.

Porter paced across the room. "After Veronica used me, I was hurt."

"Hurt?" Will said. "You were a basket case."

"A ticking bomb," Buck added.

"Okay, I was a mess." There was no denying that Porter had lost it for a while. Veronica had been his first love and when she'd dumped him, it had felt as if she'd pushed him off the hundredth floor of a high-rise. "But this morning when I was thinking about her, I finally felt at peace."

"What do you mean?" Johnny asked.

"I realized that Veronica came into my life for a reason."

"Jeez." Conway groaned. "You're not getting sentimental now, are you?"

"Hey, I'm serious. If I hadn't had to deal with what Veronica did to me, I don't think I would have seen how special Wendy is. So I forgave Veronica for using me."

"You talked to her?" Buck asked.

"No." Porter tapped his fist against his chest. "I forgave her in here and afterward the weirdest thing happened."

"Being in this church is making you talk crazy," Conway said. "You and Wendy should have gone to Vegas and gotten married by Elvis."

"Leave him alone, Conway," Will said. "What weird thing happened?"

"It felt like a huge weight had been lifted off me and the love I feel for Wendy is stronger today than it was yesterday. She's the woman for me."

"Then why the sober face?" Mack asked.

"I'm worried her parents' disapproval will affect our marriage."

"If you work hard to make Morning Sunshine Ranch a success, they'll have no choice but to accept you," Johnny said.

"Love beats out hard work. You show Wendy's folks how much you love their daughter day in and day out and you'll win them over," Will said.

"Speaking of parents," Johnny said, "has Buddy gotten the results from the paternity test?"

"Buddy will tell me as soon as he knows anything."

A throat clearing interrupted the conversation. Hat in hand, Buddy stood in the doorway of the groom's waiting room.

"I can save the news for later if you want," Buddy said.

Porter felt Johnny's hand clamp down on his shoulder and was grateful for the support. "Are you my father?"

"Yes."

Porter felt light-headed and leaned against his brother.

"You okay?" Johnny asked.

"Yeah." His gaze connected with Buddy's, and the tears shining in his father's eyes touched him. At that moment he was both happy for himself and sad for his brothers that they'd never know their own fathers or have the opportunity to form relationships with them.

"I'm not here to put any pressure on you." Buddy gestured toward Porter's brothers. "Your brothers have done a fine job helping to raise you and they were there for you when I wasn't." Buddy rubbed his eyes. "I was just hoping you'd let me be a part of your life wherever you think you can fit me in."

Johnny stepped forward. "You're right. You weren't there for Porter. We were. But if any of our dads had stepped forward and wanted to get to know us and be involved in our lives, you can damn bet we'd have jumped at the opportunity." Johnny faced Porter. "If you want to accept Buddy as your father, we'll welcome him into our family and treat him like one of our own."

Porter switched his attention to Buddy. "I'd like you to be my father."

Buddy grinned. "I was hoping you'd feel that way."

The Cash brothers took turns shaking Buddy's hand.

Before Buddy left, he said, "You all have mixed feelings about your mama, but I know she'd be proud of the men you've become."

"Thank you," Porter said.

Buddy put on his hat, then spoke over his shoulder as he made his way to the door. "I'm fifty-eight years old. Don't make me wait too long for a grandchild."

The word *grandchild* reminded Porter that although things with Buddy appeared to be on the right track, he and Wendy had a lot of work to do to bring her parents on board with their marriage. Wendy had put on a brave face when she'd told Porter that his love would be enough if her parents never accepted him. But it wasn't enough for Porter. He'd hound Mr. and Mrs. Chin every day for the rest of his life until they gave in and accepted his marriage to their daughter.

The door opened, and Mrs. Bugler poked her head inside. "Gentlemen, we're ready for you."

"I can't believe it," Buck said. "In a few short minutes the last single Cash brother is biting the dust."

Mack chuckled. "We had a hell of run, didn't we?"

"A lot of good rodeo memories," Will said.

"Remember all those nights in the bars listening to Mack's band and dancing with pretty buckle bunnies?" Conway smiled.

"And," Johnny said, "none of us would go back there for anything in the world, because we all got our happy-ever-afters with the women of our dreams."

Porter led his brothers to the altar, where they lined up facing the congregation. The front pews were filled with Cash kids and restless babies held by neighbors and friends. Mrs. Bugler played the organ, and the chapel doors opened. As matron of honor, Dixie led the procession of bridesmaids—Shannon, Beth, Isi, Marsha and Destiny. The women wore blue dresses in various styles and their husbands' faces glowed with pride and love as the ladies lined up across from them.

A church member pushed Pastor Bugler's wheelchair up to the altar. Marsha and Will had talked the older man into continuing his cancer treatments, and today the pastor's eyes were bright and his smile warm. Marsha had told Porter that her father had been looking forward to the ceremony and his spirits were high.

Porter checked out the crowd and was pleased by the number of people attending the wedding on short notice. Several pews were filled with the brothers' rodeo buddies and the entire town of Stagecoach had filed through the church doors—he supposed they had to see for themselves that the last Cash brother was getting hitched. He wished Wendy's parents were here to see that the community approved of him marrying their daughter.

The organ music switched to "The Wedding March," and Porter's heart beat faster. Heads swiveled to the back of the church and his breath froze in his lungs when the bride appeared. Wendy's gown hugged her curves and tiny waist, and his thoughts took a turn to later, after the reception, when he could have her all to himself. Then the most amazing thing happened: Wendy's mother and father joined her and escorted Wendy up the aisle. They stopped in front of Pastor Bugler, and he asked, "Who gives this bride away?"

"We do." His future in-laws' voices rang loud and clear.

"Don't you dare cry." Johnny nudged Porter's arm.

"You'll have everyone in the church bawling their heads off if you do."

Tears shone in Wendy's eyes when her father kissed her cheek, then took her hand and placed it in Porter's. "My daughter loves you," he said. "As long as you continue to make her happy, we welcome you to the family."

As far as unconditional acceptance, Mr. Chin's words left a lot to be desired. But the fact that he and his wife had shown up at the wedding to give Wendy away made Porter more than willing to meet him halfway. "You have my solemn promise that I'll honor your daughter and love her until the day I die." Mr. Chin nodded, then took his wife by the arm and led her to their seats.

"Dearly beloved, we are gathered here today..."

The pastor's words faded as Porter gazed into Wendy's eyes and envisioned waking up in the morning with her in his arms.

Yep. Life was good. Better than good. His life with Wendy would be an amazing journey. He glanced up at the ceiling, imagining Grandma Ada hovering over the Cash clan.

You'd be proud of us, Grandma. We all landed good women—women like you.

* * * * *

Watch for Marin's next
Harlequin American Romance series,
COWBOYS OF THE RIO GRANDE,
coming June 2015!

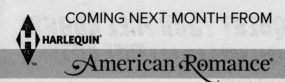
#1533 THE TWINS' RODEO RIDER
Bridesmaids Creek • by Tina Leonard
Cisco Grant's heart belongs to Suz Hawthorne, but the
people of Bridesmaids Creek have determined he is meant
for another! Can he win the woman of his dreams—and still
save the town's matchmaking reputation?

#1534 LONE STAR VALENTINE
McCabe Multiples • by Cathy Gillen Thacker
Lily McCabe is forced to ask her unrequited love, former
law school classmate Gannon Montgomery, for emergency
help when her four-year-old son's biological father sues
her for custody. Can Lily and her old flame keep things
just professional?

#1535 THE COWBOY'S VALENTINE
Crooked Valley Ranch • by Donna Alward
It's only temporary. That's what Quinn Solomon keeps telling
himself about staying at Lacey Duggan's ranch. The woman
drives him crazy! But then things really heat up between
them at the Valentine's Day dance...

#1536 KISSED BY A COWBOY
by Pamela Britton
Jillian Thacker and Wes Landon should be a match made in
heaven...except Jillian is terrified of commitment, and Wes
needs her to love him—and his baby daughter, too. Is that
two hearts too many?

REQUEST YOUR FREE BOOKS!
2 FREE NOVELS PLUS 2 FREE GIFTS!

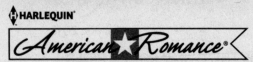

HARLEQUIN®

American ★ Romance®

LOVE, HOME & HAPPINESS

YES! Please send me 2 FREE Harlequin® American Romance® novels and my 2 FREE gifts (gifts are worth about $10). After receiving them, if I don't wish to receive any more books, I can return the shipping statement marked "cancel." If I don't cancel, I will receive 4 brand-new novels every month and be billed just $4.74 per book in the U.S. or $5.24 per book in Canada. That's a savings of at least 14% off the cover price! It's quite a bargain! Shipping and handling is just 50¢ per book in the U.S. and 75¢ per book in Canada.* I understand that accepting the 2 free books and gifts places me under no obligation to buy anything. I can always return a shipment and cancel at any time. Even if I never buy another book, the two free books and gifts are mine to keep forever.

154/354 HDN F4YN

Name _____ (PLEASE PRINT)

Address _____ Apt. #

City _____ State/Prov. _____ Zip/Postal Code

Signature (if under 18, a parent or guardian must sign)

Mail to the **Harlequin® Reader Service:**
IN U.S.A.: P.O. Box 1867, Buffalo, NY 14240-1867
IN CANADA: P.O. Box 609, Fort Erie, Ontario L2A 5X3

Want to try two free books from another line?
Call 1-800-873-8635 or visit www.ReaderService.com.

* Terms and prices subject to change without notice. Prices do not include applicable taxes. Sales tax applicable in N.Y. Canadian residents will be charged applicable taxes. Offer not valid in Quebec. This offer is limited to one order per household. Not valid for current subscribers to Harlequin American Romance books. All orders subject to credit approval. Credit or debit balances in a customer's account(s) may be offset by any other outstanding balance owed by or to the customer. Please allow 4 to 6 weeks for delivery. Offer available while quantities last.

Your Privacy—The Harlequin® Reader Service is committed to protecting your privacy. Our Privacy Policy is available online at www.ReaderService.com or upon request from the Harlequin Reader Service.

We make a portion of our mailing list available to reputable third parties that offer products we believe may interest you. If you prefer that we not exchange your name with third parties, or if you wish to clarify or modify your communication preferences, please visit us at www.ReaderService.com/consumerschoice or write to us at Harlequin Reader Service Preference Service, P.O. Box 9062, Buffalo, NY 14269. Include your complete name and address.

HAR13R

SPECIAL EXCERPT FROM

H HARLEQUIN

American Romance

Read on for a sneak peek at
THE TWINS' RODEO RIDER
by USA TODAY bestselling author Tina Leonard,
part of the **BRIDESMAIDS CREEK** *miniseries.*

"Kiss me." He leaned close to the window to give her prime access.

"Why would I want to do that?" Suz's blue eyes widened.

"Because I have nice lips. Or so I've been told. Pucker up, dollface."

"I don't pucker for anyone who calls me 'dollface,' unless you want me to look like I bit into a grapefruit. Now *that* kind of pucker may be available to you."

He laughed. "So much sass, so little honesty."

She sniffed. "I'm trying to *save* you, cowboy, not romance you. Don't confuse this."

He sighed. "No kiss? I really feel like I need to know if you're the woman of my dreams, if you're determined to win me. And a kiss tells all."

"Oh, wow." Suz looked incredulous. "You really let that line out of your mouth?"

"Slid out easily. Come on, cupcake." He closed some distance between her face and his in case she changed her mind. *Strike while the branding iron was hot* was a very worthwhile strategy. It was in fact his favorite strategy.

"If I kiss you, I probably won't like it. And then what motivation do I have to win the race? I'd just toss you back into the pond for Daisy."

He drew back, startled. "That wouldn't be good."

Suz nodded. "It could be horrible. You could be a wet kisser. Eww."

"I really don't think I am." His ego took a small dent.

"You could be a licky-kisser."

"Pretty sure I'm just right, like Goldilock's bed," he said, his ego somewhere down around his boots and flailing like a leaf on the ground in the breeze.

"I don't know," Suz said thoughtfully. "Friends don't let friends kiss friends."

"I'm not that good of a friend."

"You really want a kiss, don't you?"

He perked up at these heartening words that seemed to portend a softening in her stance. "I sure do."

"Hope you get someone to kiss you one day, then. See you around, Cisco. And don't forget, one week until the swim!"

Don't miss
THE TWINS' RODEO RIDER
by USA TODAY bestselling author Tina Leonard!

Available February 2015,
wherever Harlequin® American Romance® books
and ebooks are sold.

www.Harlequin.com

HARLEQUIN®

A *Romance* FOR EVERY MOOD™

JUST CAN'T GET ENOUGH?

Join our social communities
and talk to us online.

You will have access to the latest
news on upcoming titles and special
promotions, but most importantly,
you can talk to other fans about your
favorite Harlequin reads.

Harlequin.com/Community

Facebook.com/HarlequinBooks

Twitter.com/HarlequinBooks

Pinterest.com/HarlequinBooks

HARLEQUIN®

A *Romance* FOR EVERY MOOD™

Stay up-to-date on all your
romance-reading news with the
Harlequin Shopping Guide,
featuring bestselling authors, exciting new
miniseries, books to watch and more!

The newest issue will be delivered right to you
with our compliments! There are 4 each year.

Signing up is easy.

EMAIL

ShoppingGuide@Harlequin.ca

WRITE TO US

HARLEQUIN BOOKS
Attention: Customer Service Department
P.O. Box 9057, Buffalo, NY 14269-9057

OR PHONE

1-800-873-8635 in the United States
1-888-343-9777 in Canada

Please allow 4-6 weeks for delivery of the first issue by mail.

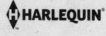